THE VINE AND THE OLIVE

Books by Margaret Culkin Banning

A Handmaid of the Lord
Pressure
The Women of the Family
Mixed Marriage
Money of Her Own
Prelude to Love
Path of True Love
The Third Son
The First Woman
The Iron Will
Letters to Susan
The Case for Chastity
You Haven't Changed
Too Young to Marry
Out in Society
Enough to Live on
A Week in New York
Salud! a South American Journal
Letters from England
Conduct Yourself Accordingly
The Clever Sister
Give Us Our Years
Fallen Away
The Dowry
The Convert
Echo Answers
The Quality of Mercy
The Vine and the Olive

The Vine and the Olive

~~~

MARGARET CULKIN BANNING

Harper & Row, Publishers
New York, Evanston, and London

For
two families
whom I love

Thy wife shall be as a fruitful vine, thy children like olive plants about thy table.

Psalms CXXVII

150 B.C.

THE VINE AND THE OLIVE

Chapter 1

~~~

"The thing is snowballing," said Herbert Martin, "it's become serious, Angus. We can't afford to ignore it."

Angus Baird still looked as if he didn't believe what the head of his public relations department was telling him.

"You can't believe it's actually going to affect our sales," he said.

"I'm sure it will. Some of the men on the road think it has already. There's an organized campaign being whipped up to boycott Baird baby foods. The word is going around that good Catholics shouldn't buy them."

"Because Clare is heading up that birth control job?" Baird asked incredulously.

"That's what's at the bottom of it. Beyond any doubt. Clare's had a whole lot of publicity—in the news magazines as well as locally. She's not only active in this thing but she's photogenic. And all this population explosion stuff is very much in the news right now. We've had a raft of letters as you see"—he tapped the pile of them he had laid on the desk—"and at first I thought like you that it was just the work of a few cranks and the best thing was to pay no attention to it."

"I still think so. This sort of lunacy subsides of its own accord if you let it alone."

1

Martin said, "No, it's getting worse every day. Some of the letters are from nuts, but not all of them by any means. And they sing pretty much the same song. The idea is that the Baird Company shouldn't be raking in money by selling food for children while the wife of the president is going around telling people not to have more kids. Here's a sample." He picked up one of the letters and read, " 'I have stopped buying baby foods made by Baird because I cannot in conscience pour out my money to be used in an attempt to destroy the American family.' Here's another honey—'Mrs. Angus Baird objects to people having children, but what would happen to her millions and her minks if decent women took her advice. . . .' "

"Crazy," interrupted Baird, "vicious. It makes no sense!" His glance went to the silver-framed picture on his desk, and he leaned forward and turned it around so that Martin would see the photograph of a beautiful young woman with a child on her lap and three more standing around her. "Does that look as if Clare objects to having children! Four in the ten years we've been married."

"The woman who wrote that letter doesn't know Clare," said Martin, "or ever would. She's attacking an image she's set up in her own mind. Or maybe her priest set it up for her. Clare is the godless rich woman tampering with the morals of the poor. This birth control business is very emotional because it's a tangle of sex and religion. We're up against something that can do us a great deal of harm, Angus. I wish you'd take my word for it."

"You know the public better than I do. If you're so concerned about this, what do you think should be done? Perhaps some of this wretched publicity that Clare is getting ought to include more mention of her own family. To point up her real attitude, I mean."

"I thought of that. Felt it out. But for one thing, Clare won't let the children be photographed for the papers—she thinks it's corny and also bad for the children. And they always want pictures if they run a story. It might work the wrong way anyhow. I know a girl who pulls a lot of weight with the *Observer*—she practically runs the women's pages and I've often planted stories with her that fitted into our advertising. She would be glad to use pictures of Clare's family if they were available. But Clare refused. And Anne Milner said to me—she's plenty smart about public reactions—she said that a good many women would look at pictures of Clare with her children and say, 'It's all right for her. Mrs. Baird is rich and probably has half a dozen nurses to look after her children while she goes around telling other women they ought to have just so many.' There's always a grievance against the rich just under the surface. You know that. Anyway, I don't think playing up your family is the answer."

"Then what is?"

"Frankly, I think Clare ought to resign from that job."

"Give it up altogether?"

"Lay off it completely. And let it be known publicly that she is doing just that." He went on after a second as if he hadn't quite finished what he wanted to tell Baird. "The best thing would be if it got around that she resigned because she was pregnant."

"She's not," said Baird shortly, "and not going to be. This last one nearly killed her. Hell, Herb, I never wanted Clare to get mixed up with this birth control outfit. There's something embarrassing about it." He grinned ruefully and said, "Feels like an invasion of privacy. But Clare takes it very seriously. It's a kind of crusade with her. She thinks it's the answer to practically everything that's wrong with the world."

"Yes, she talked that way to me when I was at your house for dinner last week. But does she know that it's affecting your business?"

"Not unless you told her so the other night."

"I didn't. I didn't think it ought to come from me."

"I'm still not convinced that you aren't blowing this thing

up out of all proportion to its importance. Suppose we are blacklisted by a few bigots temporarily, does it matter so much? When we have the best baby foods on the market and damn well know that we have? There's no other company that's done as much research and testing. And what women want is the best product for their kids."

"Normally," Martin agreed uncontentiously, but his calmness was not yielding. "Maybe we can ride the bumps as far as our baby foods go. There are plenty of Protestant mothers. But what if the boycott spreads to our mixes? Suppose that instead of being a firm that everyone respects—and that's how Baird rates now—suppose we became public enemy number one to thousands of Catholics?"

"That's pretty far-fetched."

"I hope so. But I don't know. There's something in the air that we have to look out for—people are more personal than they used to be. If you have any dealing with the public, they are curious about your private life."

"In politics maybe."

"In business too. The consumer is getting like the voter—he wants to know who runs the show and what he is like personally. We come up against that all the time—we use it too and often it's a help. That's why I'm inclined to believe that the Cassidy boys already have wind of this and are licking their chops. Wouldn't they like to get the edge on their chief competitors without spending a nickel? And wouldn't that burn up the members of our Board."

"You certainly don't expect me to bring this thing up at the directors' meeting this afternoon, do you?"

"Why not talk it over with Clare first?" asked Martin.

"What do you mean—'first'?"

Herbert Martin lit another cigarette and started to ramble around the room. He was a tall, thin, not quite handsome man whose face was stamped with perception. After a minute's stalking he said, "Some members of the Board have heard about this already."

4

"You've been discussing it with them!" exclaimed Baird. He was beginning to sound angry.

"I didn't bring it up. Of course I wouldn't start anything without talking to you first. But Mr. Ginn buttonholed me at the club yesterday. He was roundabout and very careful, but he said that he had heard some criticism of certain activities to which members of the families of our company were lending their names and support. He didn't mention Clare, but it was obvious that he meant this birth control thing. He asked me if I thought that public disapproval would affect us in any way. That put me up against the ax. I played dumb."

Angus Baird no longer wore an expression of bored incredulity. The mention of Mr. Ginn had washed that off his face. His public relations man had spoken of the oldest and most difficult member of the board of directors, whose opinions were hardening along with his arteries, whose name was rarely used without the prefix of "Mister" because his old-style dignity and authority demanded it.

Martin said without emphasis, "Mr. Ginn's not a Catholic. But isn't his wife one?"

There was pause enough for an unspoken decision. Martin knew his chief well enough to be sure that it had been made and that he almost certainly had won his point.

"Let's forget this for now, Herb. Bring me up to date on the Brazilian fisheries. If they are going to be a source of vitamins, can we get them at a decent price or are those bandits going to hold us up? That's on the agenda for this afternoon."

When he had been briefed on the latest developments in his firm's relation with the Brazilian fish industry and Martin had left the office, Baird looked at his watch and saw that he had a few minutes to spare before the directors would convene at three o'clock. He readjusted the photograph of his family, thinking irrelevantly, it doesn't do her justice. The oil that Crain did of her is far better, but I want her to be painted again.

Adequate or not, the photograph proved distinction and

rare beauty. There was tenderness, and amusement too, in Clare Baird's expression. Her glance seemed to have been raised from the child she was holding to meet the present scrutiny of her husband. Though the picture was black and white and showed only the lovely molding of her features and the dark hair that was never too patterned, Angus Baird saw her in color—the unpainted olive of her skin, the surprise of deeply blue eyes.

He thought, I'll get her out of this, but I'll only tell her as much as I have to. I must try to make her feel that she's not altogether to blame. Clare's not used to being before the public and she doesn't know what the score can be. I might have foreseen this sort of reaction—she never would. In the beginning I should have told her that she must keep out of a deal like this. Angus thought back but he couldn't remember exactly when he was first aware that she had become involved in the birth control movement. A year ago? It didn't matter. He said to himself, she'll be horrified about those letters and the fact that what she's doing might affect the corporation. I'll play that down.

Suddenly, because he wanted to protect her immediately, or because he wanted to be sure that she wasn't already troubled by criticism, or perhaps only to hear her voice, he lifted the telephone and dialed his home on the private line.

"Hello, Magda. Is Mrs. Baird at home?"

"No, sir," said the maid who answered, "she went out about half an hour ago."

"Do you know where I could reach her?"

"Mrs. Baird said she was going to a club meeting at the Pacific Hotel."

Baird thanked her and cradled the phone.

Anne Milner was at the end of the press table at the afternoon session of the State Federation of Women's Clubs. The gilded ballroom of the Pacific Hotel was crowded, and from

6

where she sat Anne could see both the speakers' platform and the audience of delegates. Both views bored her. Anne was reflecting, not for the first time, that a mass of middle-aged women was a depressing sight. She felt the contempt of youth —of a girl who had a date for dinner with a man who was in love with her—for women who had passed the age of romance. Most of these women were compensating for that, Anne believed. She thought, women are dreadful without men. Unless this were my job, unless I were being paid for it, nothing on earth would make me come to a club meeting.

For the last half hour the delegates had been laboriously arguing about the wording of a resolution concerned with the admission of Red China to the United Nations. As if it would make the slightest difference, Anne said to herself as they haggled. She would describe the way they fussed over this to Francis tonight—in words she certainly couldn't use in her newspaper story—and how he would laugh!

She looked at the agenda to see how long her boredom must last. Resolutions from the floor would come next, but they would not be important. No resolution which was not approved by some committee would get anywhere. This was only a gesture of democracy, to give freaks and crackpots a chance to air their views. Anne began to pile her notes together as the chairman said, "If there are any resolutions to be presented from the floor, I ask those who offer them to come to the platform so that they may be heard by everyone."

Anne knew that request would serve further to curb erratic resolutions, for many women would be too shy or unsure of themselves to mount the platform. Then with surprise she recognized the person who was already going up the steps to the ballroom stage. It was Mrs. Angus Baird. She must have come in from one of the side reception rooms. Anne had not seen her at this or any other session of the convention until now. She had not expected to see Clare Baird here. If it were a horse show or a Junior League benefit . . . she's probably here on some Junior League job, Anne decided. She's gone all out for birth control in the last year, but she couldn't bring that up at this meeting. Anne watched Clare Baird with pleasure, admiring the raspberry-colored suit that a master hand had tailored, approving the warm, gracious voice that wasn't a pretentious, speech-making one. Anne thought, she must be a wonderful hostess.

Clare Baird greeted the chairman and delegates and thanked them for the privilege of bringing a very important matter "before this influential group." And then, "I have come here today to represent the world-wide organization of Planned Parenthood."

Immediately Anne felt the excitement rise in the ballroom. She herself shared the sudden tension. The words of the beautiful woman on the platform fell into a listening silence. Clare Baird was speaking without notes, without wasting time and yet unhurriedly. She gave facts and figures. She was not mincing her words as she outlined the growth of population and emphasized the need to check it. Father Collins should hear this, Anne thought with secret amusement at the image of his anger. Catholic though Anne herself was, the constant preachments against birth control from the pulpit in her church often seemed excessive.

"In the few minutes allowed me," said Clare Baird, "I can only scratch the surface of this subject. But I believe that no woman—and no man—can consider even these few figures and remain indifferent to the crises that are mounting all over the world. The human race is breeding itself into certain misery and great danger. We all know that poverty, famine and lack of living space are major causes of wars. If the population explosion is not checked, we shall encourage war by sheer lack of precaution. And even worse than war is life at such a low level that it degrades human beings. If we ignore what is happening, we allow—actually we're promoting—that kind of life.

"This isn't a remote problem. In China, Central and South

America and Egypt the growth of population is appalling. But we are facing trouble right here at home. The computers tell us that in forty-six years our population of one hundred and eighty million will double if the present birth rate is maintained. Perhaps there will not be famine here. But there will not be enough schools or teachers. There will be twice as many pupils within the lifetime of our children, and we all worry because the educational system is so hard-pressed now. The same problem will confront the hospitals. Traffic will become a horror.

"Overcrowding," Clare Baird went on, speaking without dramatizing what she was saying, "is never good for people, whether it is in a room, or in a country or in the world. It means that the weaker ones are pushed and shoved. It means that no one is comfortable. In overcrowded places nothing is adequate or even safe. Basically it is the woman's job to do something about this. We bear the children—we should decide how many can be cared for. What is at stake is the quality of our life. We must teach women—especially the forlorn, underprivileged ones—that children who will have no chance of a healthy, decent life must not be born."

There was the sharp sound of a hiss. Anne looked quickly in the direction from where it had come, but she could not be sure which of several stony-faced women in that corner had made the ugly noise.

A flashbulb went off and Anne saw that it was Charley Ross, from her own newspaper, who was taking a picture of the speaker. That was fine, a good break. He had probably been sent over to take a picture of the incoming officers and arrived just at the right time. There would be a photograph of the beautiful Mrs. Angus Baird to print with her story of this, and if there was a fight over the resolution and she dramatized it well enough, it might make the front page.

Clare Baird had paid no attention to the hiss or the flash of the camera. She went on with her argument for a minute or two more and then, lifting a card in her hand, she read, "Madam President, I move the adoption of the following resolution. Resolved that the federated clubs assembled here in convention on September 10, 1963, being aware of the dangers of uncontrolled population, commend the study of responsible parenthood to their various units and urge them to take action in their communities to promote the planning of parenthood."

She stepped back but did not leave the platform. The chairman, a big woman breasted with orchids, came quickly to the rostrum as the crowd stirred and murmured audibly.

"Is there a second to this motion?"

Several women were already on their feet. One shrill voice came first.

"Madam Chairman, I protest the introduction of this resolution and move that no consideration be given it by this convention."

"Second!"

"Madam Chairman, I second the resolution."

"Second the motion to disregard it."

"I rise to a point of order. There is a motion before the house!"

"Madam Chairman—"

The session that had been so dull had become a babel of excited interruptions and voices in conflict. They are no longer clubwomen, thought Anne. They are wives and mothers and each one of them has her own secret sex experience. They are thinking of their men and their children—the ones they didn't want or couldn't have or are proud of having because it gives them a reason for living. Some of them are furious because Mrs. Angus Baird in her—I'll bet it is—Dior suit is telling them what they would like to do, but they are afraid they'll go to hell if they do it. A good many of them apparently want to go along with her. She might just put this over.

A woman with a face as worn and undistinguished as her

clothes now had the floor. Anne had never seen her before. But as soon as she began to speak, her serenity and dignity pulled together the scattered attention of the meeting.

"Madam Chairman, this resolution may be well intentioned —I believe it is—but it is ill advised. How can this convention commend to its member clubs practices which to many individuals are sinful? The sponsor of the resolution has stated that women should decide how many children should be born to them—and to others. There are many in this room and more in our organization who disagree and believe that God should make that decision. There are many who believe that it is presumption to imagine that we know whether children should be born."

There was a burst of applause, but the speaker lifted her hand to check it. "Please, let us not end this wonderful meeting on any note of contention. But Madam Chairman, if I may have one more minute, I would like to tell a simple story."

The harassed chairman nodded consent.

"It concerns two doctors. One said to the other, 'I would like to have your opinion about the termination of a pregnancy. . . .' "

How alive the room feels, thought Anne. That word "pregnancy" does it.

" 'The father,' explained the doctor who was asking for an opinion, 'was syphilitic, the mother tubercular. Of four children already born to them, one was blind, the second died, the third was deaf and dumb, the fourth became tubercular. What would you have done about the fifth pregnancy?' The other doctor said, 'Of course I would have ended it.' But the first replied, 'Then you would have murdered Beethoven.' "

The speaker sat down in the midst of a hush. Quickly another woman broke it.

"I support this resolution. It seems to me high time that organizations which claim that they want to be useful to the world take their heads out of the sand and become realistic. It

11

is possibly better to do without a Beethoven than to fill our institutions with feeble-minded, helpless, useless beings."

The frantic waving for recognition began again.

"I think we must limit this discussion," said the chairman. "We have several other items of business on the agenda."

"Question!"

"You have heard the resolution. All those in favor of its adoption will please signify by raising their hands."

Hands went up, some boldly high, some seeming uncertain. Ushers went up and down the aisles, counting. For a minute it looked to Anne as if the resolution might have a chance.

"Opposed."

No—it was lost. Evidently not only the Catholic women were voting against it. Anne recognized many women who did not belong to her faith but had their hands in the air now. That figures, she thought. They don't think the subject should be aired, or are afraid it will start a civil war in their clubs if they sponsor it—or perhaps they don't think Clare Baird, who certainly isn't a rank-and-file clubwoman, has any right to barge into their show. Yet they probably practice birth control themselves—or did when it was necessary. And plenty of Catholic women do too, or we wouldn't hear so much about it from the altar. If I had to vote on this . . . She found herself suddenly wondering what she would do—she didn't have a vote, so why worry?

"The resolution is lost."

With a resumed feeling of distaste for all these women, Anne gathered up the notes for her story and left the ballroom through one of the nearest doors. As she drove her little coupe out of the parking lot she saw Clare Baird come out of the hotel alone and unlock a sports car that gleamed with cost. There's nothing she can't have, thought Anne, except what she just couldn't get in that ballroom. The nationally familiar picture of a pink-cheeked smiling baby that was featured in so many Baird advertisements came into Anne's mind. She

12

thought, there's something a little ironic about Clare Baird telling people to limit their families. She's working against her husband's interests.

At seven o'clock Anne met Francis Dearborn. It was Friday and so they had chosen a seafood restaurant for dinner. It overlooked the lake, and the last hour of sunset was painting the water as they sat down at a table beside one of the windows. They were consciously happy—the beginning of an evening together was always both relaxing and exciting.

The features and physique of Francis Dearborn had been passed down to him from Irish ancestors and he did them credit. They must have been dark-skinned Celts—Francis had told Anne that his great-grandfather came from the Aran Islands, where Spanish ships had been wrecked and Spanish sailors cast ashore. There was natural gallantry in his manner and he could add a touch of mockery that was sometimes bewildering in the courtroom. Often some witness could not be sure whether or not this flattering lawyer was taking him for a ride. Francis was, Anne knew, somewhat conceited. But she did not mind that. It was a pleasant, male conceit of the kind as necessary to some men as shaving soap.

Anne had been pressed for time, but she had found enough to make herself lovely. She had beauty that could be dramatized or played down. This afternoon at the meeting she had not made anyone look at her twice, but tonight glances sought her out, lingered and came back. She liked to surprise and delight Francis with a new dress, a different hairdo, deliberate carelessness or perfect grooming. Now she wore sheer-white wool because almost all women dining in restaurants wore black.

"What's it made of—cumulus?" asked Francis.

They were not formally promised to each other yet. Anne knew that she would probably marry Francis Dearborn, but she was delaying the decision and enjoying the delay. Marriage would mean the end of provocative meetings like this and Anne was not ready to exchange courtship for domesticity.

While they were drinking cocktails and through the pleasantly long dinner she told him about the meeting, caricaturing the desperation of the chairman. Dearborn was amused. He liked to listen to Anne threading the story on ripples of laughter. He liked her wit, the rebel in her that was just under the surface. When her talk was frank and unexpurgated, he was often most conscious of her innocence. She was not a docile companion, but her instinctive resistance to any kind of bridle was challenging to a man, sometimes amusing, often charming. Francis Dearborn, like Anne herself, was in no immediate hurry for marriage. When he was given another boost in salary by his law firm, as was sure to happen before too long, he intended to insist that Anne marry him. He would not let this girl get away. But a man with a family took on a big load. If a man was too young or not well established, it could be crushing. Time enough, no matter what his mother said. Watching Anne with pleasure, Francis thought of his mother fondly scolding, "You're past thirty. You should be married. There've been too many selfish old bachelors in this family." She needn't worry. He wasn't going to be a bachelor. When he was ready . . .

Anne was saying, "Clare Baird is very intelligent. Besides being beautiful. Brains and beauty and so much money that she can have anything she wants—it's almost too much for one woman, hardly fair."

"Funny thing, though," said Francis, "a woman in her position getting up before the public and talking on a subject like that. I should think it would embarrass her husband. He's very prominent, and very well liked. I don't know him personally, but I undoubtedly will in the future, for our firm handles some of the legal work for his corporation. I shouldn't think that Baird would let his wife put on a performance like that."

"She doesn't seem like the kind of woman who would be let or not let."

"It seems unnatural—not feminine—for a woman not to want children."

"Oh, that's not it, Fran. She has four of her own."

"Then what's she on the warpath for?"

"She believes that the world is headed for trouble. There are going to be too many people in the world for things to go around. Even in this country. You should have heard some of the figures she gave!"

"I've seen the figures. They're tricky. A lot of them are guesswork. Of course population is on the increase everywhere. That's not news. It's bound to happen because so many diseases are being stamped out. Life is more comfortable, less perilous than it used to be."

"According to what she says, it won't be comfortable very long if women go on having children more or less at random."

"That's not a thing you can dictate for other people. Not Mrs. Baird or anyone else. You say the crowd turned down her proposition. There it is."

"Yes, they did, but they'll go home . . . Women are such hypocrites!"

"Are they? I've often wondered."

She was serious. "Most of the ones who know how practice birth control when they want to. Even many of the Catholic women. If they didn't, we wouldn't hear so much about it from the altar."

"That's a good point. But there's a Catholic way."

"It's not very reliable."

Francis smiled, remembering that a friend of his had said that the rhythm method was playing Russian roulette in bed.

"What makes you smile?"

"A crazy remark I heard someone make came into my head. Not for your ears, not now. I'll tell you some day. But the long and short of it is that people have to work these things out for themselves."

"I suppose they should. But do they? Can they? Even my sister Joyce—" Anne broke off whatever she had started to say.

15

"Joyce and Chris are happy, aren't they?"

"Oh yes, nobody more than those two."

"And they want a large family apparently. Nobody has any right to tell them how many children they should have. It's their own business."

"Of course," said Anne. She thought, I'm sure that Joyce lives in terror of having more children. But she never admits it.

"You really don't think there's any danger of overpopulating the earth?" she asked, swinging back to the general subject as safer.

"I think the danger is greatly exaggerated. It's certainly not serious in North America. We have a growing economy. We have to keep the farmers from producing food, and even then we have surpluses in the grain elevators that are political headaches."

"Yes, but Clare Baird said this afternoon that even in this country we'll be short of schools and doctors and lots of necessary things in less than fifty years."

"I'm inclined to doubt the lady. Shortages correct themselves. Supply catches up with demand. You don't want to let these propagandists scare you, you beautiful girl in your white cloud."

The compliment was to divert her from argument. Anne knew that most men—and Francis more than most—disliked having a conversation with a woman become a debate.

"All right," she said, "I won't let them scare me."

"Tell you what. When we get ready to have a family, we'll get a place in the country and raise our own potatoes. And keep cows—and goats—so we'll be sure to have milk for the children."

"When," said Anne, now smiling at him over the rim of her glass, teasing him in return.

"I'm very much in love with you—more all the time," he said.

When he spoke like that, with the desire for possession in his voice, Anne felt a quick response in her own senses. She was afraid of it tonight. There were times like this when her body was eager and her mind reluctant.

"I don't like to be very far away from you even for a few days," said Francis, "do you know that?"

"I didn't. It's lovely to know. I shall think of it tomorrow."

It was a sweet promise. He said, "Anne, when I come back—"

"How long are you going to be away?"

"I hope not longer than the weekend."

"Is it a very important trip?"

"It can be very important. To me as well as the firm and some of our clients. Every law firm that handles corporation business has a member who takes care of the political angles. I think they may be grooming me for that."

"You'd like that?"

"It could lead to anything, Anne. To very important connections. Confidentially, I expect to see the Governor tomorrow."

"Then you must go home and to bed so that you'll be fine and fresh and clever. How did it ever get to be after ten o'clock? We seem to be closing this place. Shall we go?"

"Back to your apartment for an hour?"

She hesitated, then said with flattering regret, "Not tonight, Fran. You have a big day tomorrow. And I have my car."

"You mean that?"

"Yes, I really do—tonight."

"Well, if that's the way you want it." It was better, he too knew that. Francis signaled the waiter, who was hovering restlessly, with his eye on their table. He had brought fresh pots of coffee twice. "I'll put you in your car and call you when I get home to be sure that you're all right."

The light burning on the porch of the house which had been the home of the Dearborn family for sixty years showed it for what it was—substantial enough to last that long, undistinguished and capacious. It was a good property, and growing more valuable in its old age, because it was no longer on the far edge of the city and gas stations and supermarkets were creeping up on it greedily. The large plate-glass front window, heavily shadowed by the roof of the porch, and the minor windows of the hallway and dining room were still curtained with Brussels lace, as they had been when Anthony Dearborn brought his bride to the house as mistress. That was thirty-five years ago. Mrs. Dearborn had replaced the curtains twice but never changed the material or style. Nothing else would have seemed natural to her on those windows, as nothing except the square dome of colored glass which hung over the oak dining-room table would have seemed to belong there.

Francis Dearborn knew tolerantly that his home was very old-fashioned and out-of-date. But it served his purposes and could do so a little longer. He did not bring his social or business life here. There were clubs and restaurants that could be used for that. And the old house was comfortable. He had installed a new oil burner a few years ago in place of the coal-burning furnace and rewired most of the rooms for safety. There was a washing machine in the basement now and a modern refrigerator in the back entry. His mother refused to let him buy her a mangle because, as she said, there was nothing like them to wear out good linen. Nor did she want a dishwasher. But she had finally graduated from the old radio to the companionship of television. She was sitting before the set in the back parlor when Francis fitted his key in the door. He hung his coat on one of the prongs of the hatrack and came in to say good night to her.

"Anything good on tonight?" he asked.

"Silly stuff mostly. I was waiting for the news."

Mrs. Dearborn was always ashamed of getting interested in things completely remote from her own sensible, virtuous life. Tonight the Paris fashions had been fascinatingly scandalous and the drama of a ruthless criminal so unbelievable that she was watching Part Two.

"Turn if off, dear," she said, "turn the sound down anyway till it's time for the news and the weather. I hope you'll have a good day tomorrow for your flight."

He twisted the knob and the picture went on silently. Mrs. Dearborn did not completely ignore it.

She said, "I packed your shirts and socks and underthings. You can put the rest that you want to take with you in the suitcase tomorrow morning."

"Thanks, Mother, that's fine."

"Have you had a nice evening?"

"Yes, very pleasant. Had dinner at the Harbor Inn."

"With Anne, I expect?"

"That's a very good guess."

"Have you put a sparkler on her finger yet?"

"Now, Mother—don't you begin that."

"You don't listen to me anyhow."

He smiled at her affectionately and lit a cigarette.

She was no longer a pretty woman. Her cheeks had broadened and over-softened and her neck was bent a little from hours over the ironing board and the kitchen sink that had always been too low. But it was a wise face. Her glance at her son gave him both affection and slightly critical observation.

"Well, of course it's in the blood," she said.

"What is?"

"Your attitude," she said, "toward marriage. It's a strange thing to be handed on from one generation to another. And retained in a world where there are such wild and unholy goings-on as you can see on that screen. But maybe you can't help yourself."

"Mother, that in-the-blood stuff is just so much nonsense. I know what I want to do."

"You may not know why you want it."

"Are you going in for psychiatry now?"

"Hardly that. But we're a curious race, the Irish."

"We're not Irish. We're Americans and have been for more than two generations. My grandfather came over when he was only a boy and he married a girl whose family had already been here for a long time."

"But he married a girl of Irish descent. That's the way it's been in this family. When the men marry, they don't change the blood or the religion. Look at yourself, the girl you seem to have picked out and now keep waiting."

"I don't think of Anne as Irish. Or as kept waiting."

She had stopped watching the picture. She said, "Well, you had better get on with it. It's in your nature to put it off. To enjoy the liberty you have. To keep yourself to yourself. There's a broad streak of selfishness in this family, and I say it with all respect to those who have taken Holy Orders."

"What do you mean by that crack?" he asked with amusement.

"Look at it," said Mrs. Dearborn, "my own family. There were eight of the Hayes children, seven who lived. You know how they came out. Two of them priests, one still surviving. And Veronica was determined to enter the convent. John and Stephen never married—without reason, for they were handsome—and Barbara had to do their housekeeping, or thought she did, so she stayed single till she died. I was the only one to marry."

"Then you have nothing to blame yourself for," he told her.

"I don't blame myself. But I blame your father—I blame Tony Dearborn for keeping me waiting fifteen years. I was twenty-two when I met him first. I was thirty-seven when we married. Fifteen years I corrected papers and taught reading and washed blackboards in the fourth-grade room at the Washington School when I should have been washing diapers for my own children. Your brothers and sisters should have been born in those fifteen years."

"Why didn't you marry if you felt that way?"

20

"Tony felt there was no hurry. So did his mother. There is something ferocious about some of the Irish mothers, and she wasn't so far from the soil as we were on my side of the family. I learned my lesson from her. She did not want to give up her son to me. And she would not have, even if I had been willing to live with her."

"So it wasn't until after she died you could marry."

"Not till then. Then he brought me to this house. I loved your father—I never had eyes for any other man—but some of the bloom was off and I was middle-aged and approaching the change. I was lucky to be able to bear one child."

"And now you're trying to chase him out," said Francis.

She would not let him make a joke of it. She said, "You're well enough fixed to get married and start raising your own family. But there's a strange resistance among the Irish, more in the men than in the women. I read it somewhere—there's a natural liking for celibacy in Irishmen. Little of the urge to increase and multiply. A streak of selfishness, as I said before."

"Look, Mother, get this straight. I don't consider myself Irish."

"No, you do not live in Ireland," said Mrs. Dearborn. "There comes the news, dear. And after it comes the weather with the Puroil man. Turn it up again."

Chapter 2

✺

Angus Baird sat down at the breakfast table and looked with satisfaction at the perfect ripeness of the melon that Magda had placed before him. He unfolded the morning newspaper which lay beside his plate. Then as he took a look at the front page he said, "My God! What's this!"

No one answered. The maid had left the room to get the coffee and Clare was still in the small dining room, where the children had their meals except on special occasions. Her own place was waiting for her opposite her husband and soon she would join him as usual. The arrangement had been planned to allow him an undisturbed breakfast.

But this one was going to be worse than disturbed. Anne Milner's story had been printed on the front page as she had hoped it might be. It was flanked by a two-column picture of Clare on the platform, and the entire feature was topped by headlines reading

WOMEN REJECT BIRTH CONTROL PLEA
OF SOCIALITE

MRS. ANGUS BAIRD FAILS TO
CONVINCE 1200 CLUBWOMEN THAT
CURB MUST BE PUT ON FAMILIES

Baird read on with a sickened feeling, remembering everything that Martin had told him yesterday. He had intended to talk to Clare about the matter last night. But they had gone to a dinner party, and when they came home, she had been so beautiful and so dear that he only wanted to make love to her. As he had done. He had promised himself that he would tell her this morning what Martin was so worried about. His own concern had lessened overnight and he was swinging back to the hope that the whole matter was exaggerated. But here it was, staring him in the face, plastered all over the front page. Even if he had taken it up with Clare, he couldn't have prevented this. Herb should have done something about this before yesterday, he thought angrily. Baird's glance reverted to the by-line. *By Anne Milner.* That was the name of the girl Herb Martin had mentioned—a hussy looking for a sensation.

Clare came in, paused as she passed Angus to leave a light kiss on his hair. She too had been very happy last night.

He said in a tone of cold disgust, "Will you look at this?"

Clare glanced at the paper over his shoulder.

"A convention of women from all parts of the state turned down an ardent plea for birth control made by Mrs. Angus Baird," he read aloud.

"But the vote was closer than we expected it would be," Clare said, "and it was something just to get the resolution before that big crowd. I think if some of those women hadn't been afraid to vote as they really feel—"

He slammed the newspaper down and half rose, staring at his wife. Clare stopped talking and went to her place at the head of the table in silence.

"What in heaven's name has got into you, Clare? Aren't you ashamed of this? Do you like this horrible publicity—a person in your position! Doesn't it make you even squirm?"

She said slowly, "Of course I don't like it. For myself. I try not to let it make me squirm—I have to. Because we need publicity. We have to make people think about the situation—face up to it."

"My wife—talking about sex for the newspapers, about what people are up to in bed—"

"Angus, please!"

Magda came in with the silver tray. Angus Baird grimly attacked his melon. Clare poured the coffee and said, "I'll ring, Magda, when Mr. Baird is ready for his eggs."

The door to the butler's pantry closed and Baird stopped eating. He said, "You've got to get out of this business, Clare. I don't know what harm's been done, but that can't be helped now. We'll have to weather that. The only thing that can be done now is for you to sever all connection with this racket or whatever it is and hope to God that people will forget that you were ever mixed up in it."

Clare said, "I'm terribly sorry that it bothers you so much, Angus. I know you don't like to have personal things about us in the newspapers and I've tried to keep them out. I wouldn't have meetings here at the house or let them take pictures of the children—"

"It's encouraging to know you stopped at something," he said, "but this female brawl you got yourself into yesterday is going to make a lot of talk. I don't know if Herb Martin can soft-pedal it in any way and keep it from being quoted. Anyway, lie low yourself. Maybe you might slip out of town for a few weeks, go down to the lodge. And there's no necessity for giving any reason for your resignation—except that you can't give it any more of your time."

"But Angus, I can't possibly resign—"

"Why not?"

"Because I've promised to do so many things. I'm speaking in quite a lot of places—and there's the national meeting in Philadelphia in January—and don't you understand that I want to do this? It's important, Angus, it's the most important thing—"

24

"More important than your husband's business? The Baird Company?"

"Your business hasn't anything to do with it."

"Some people think it has. We sell baby foods. Letters have been coming into the office protesting your part in this birth control propaganda."

"I know. I've had some of those fantastic letters at headquarters—I put them in the wastebasket. They make no sense—"

"They make sense enough to have started a boycott of Baird Baby Foods—"

"Oh no—"

"Herb Martin doesn't put those letters in the wastebasket—he came to me yesterday with a lot of them and he's worried. He says you must get out of this completely. And fast."

"I'll explain to him that it would be quite impossible. I'll talk to Herb. Shall I ring for your eggs?"

"I don't want any eggs," he said, crumpling his napkin and tossing it on the table. "What I want is your promise that you will break your connection with this thing immediately. And permanently." He got up from his chair, took a few steps toward her end of the table and stood there, looking at her, waiting. He remembered last night again. He thought, I mustn't blow my top like this. She just doesn't realize what this could involve. She's had no experience. He said, quietly now, "You must take my judgment in this matter, dear."

"If I could . . ."

She's beginning to want to, Angus thought. And he went on, "It's not womanly to expose yourself to the public like this. Especially on such a subject. It's not a thing a woman like you—in your position—argues about in front of strangers. They misunderstand why you do it—they attribute cheap motives to you. I know you meant well, Clare, but you must see that you can't go on with it."

"It doesn't matter what anyone thinks my motives are," said Clare. "People have to be told the facts."

"But not by you."

"I said I would help. I took it on. Angus, I can't believe that this will really do your business any harm."

"Herb is dead-sure that it will. Already has. He believes that what you've been doing is already helping our competitors."

"Don't you think he may be exaggerating the situation because of his job? Because he's so sensitive to all your public relations?"

"I wanted to think so. But he's not the only one. Mr. Ginn tackled Herb about it."

"Mr. Ginn did?" Clare was silent for half a minute and then said, "He's a very reactionary old man."

"He owns a great deal of Baird stock, reactionary or not."

"And his wife—you know she's a really bigoted Catholic. She made a terrible row because her granddaughter was going to be a bridesmaid at a wedding in a Protestant church, and the poor girl had to drop out—"

"That's neither here nor there."

"Maybe not. I wish you'd eat some breakfast, Angus."

"I'm waiting for your promise."

"I can't promise what you want. I'd let down too many people."

"And you prefer to let your husband down?"

"Angus, Planned Parenthood isn't like other organizations. It's not a bridge club or a sewing circle. It's got a job to do—a job that has to be done, unless—"

"Spare me the speeches," he said curtly. "Are you going to go along with me or not?"

Clare said, "I'd have no respect for myself at all if I gave up a job I took on and believe has to be done because I was afraid the Baird Company would sell less baby food."

"That sounds very fine. But look at it squarely. I've got several hundred men trying to sell Baird products all over the world. Does it occur to you that they have to earn a living and that to have the wife of their boss throw a monkey wrench into their chances of making sales is outrageous?"

"That won't happen. People won't connect what I may do with their groceries."

"You don't think they did yesterday? You're spread all over the paper—as who? As Mrs. Angus Baird, wife of the president of Baird Foods, Mrs. Baird the socialite!"

If she flinched it was inwardly. Clare stayed at the head of her table, the silver gleaming around her. She was wearing a gold-striped morning dress and looked as serene as beautiful. But the fruit and coffee before her were untouched.

"You must remember that you're my wife, that our interests are the same—"

"Until . . ." She paused.

"Until you get an exhibitionist desire to go before the public?"

"You're being pretty cruel," she said in that quiet voice.

"Sorry. I know it isn't that with you. And I realize that it may be difficult and disappointing for you to bow out. But you can help with funds. And someone else can carry the ball. People soon forget—"

"I wouldn't forget. Not ever. Angus, I'm not going to bow out. I'm going to go on with what I'm doing."

He managed a surface appearance of control, trying to match her understated resistance.

"I hope not," he said grimly. "I have enough confidence in your discretion—and your loyalty—to believe you will change your mind when you think this over."

He left the room, and Clare listened to the sound of other doors closing as he went out of the house. She thought that

27

he had never left it in anger with her before, not once in their ten years of marriage.

Herbert Martin again was too late. He had not lost a minute after he read the story in getting in touch with the editor of the *Observer*. He had plenty of influence, for the Baird Company's advertising was very valuable. But he found that the Associated Press had already put a condensed story of the birth control battle at the convention on their wires. That meant that it would be published anywhere and everywhere that a newspaper editor hoped it might excite interest. The disastrous line in the story, as far as Martin was concerned, and the one that he knew would surely be used freely, was the one that identified Clare as the wife of the president of Baird Foods.

There was nothing that Martin could do now to bring back the story from the winds. He felt, bitterly, as Angus Baird had, that he should have gone to his boss and explained the danger in what Clare was doing before yesterday. He was not a man to excuse a blunder in himself, and he spent no time in doing that now. He concentrated immediately on how to minimize any unfortunate results. Nothing would help except Clare's resignation from the birth control organization. That must come at once, and the public must be made aware of it to counteract this sickening story, which Martin knew would be presently attracting notice in the quarters where it could do most harm.

He was right. Mr. Ginn took the paper into his wife's room after he had finished with it. She was a white-haired wraith of a woman, now propped up against her pillows with a breakfast tray before her. The beautiful missal from which she had already read the epistle and gospel assigned to the patron saint of this day was on her bedside table.

Mr. Ginn said, "There's a story in the paper here that I think will shock you as much as it did me."

"I can't bear to read some of those things."

"You'll want to look at this. It's about Angus Baird's wife—she's been mixed up in a public fracas over this birth control business."

His wife reached for the paper and spoke as she looked for the story, her glance held for an instant by Clare's picture.

"I can't understand it. You'd think that a woman in her position . . ."

"She was a Melander, wasn't she? One of the leading families in the whole state. Her grandfather was governor—"

"Always very worldly," said his wife, reading, "brought up their children without any religion. This is what happens. I should think Clare Baird would fear that she'd be punished by something happening to one of her own children. Think of her asking those women, right in public, to condone—"

"It certainly doesn't do the Baird firm any good to have her make a holy show of herself," said Mr. Ginn. "I've heard there's been criticism. I spoke to young Martin about the effect it might have on our customers. He was inclined to discount it. I'm going to talk to some other members of the Board about it. Angus ought to exercise some control over his wife."

Francis Dearborn did not have a chance to look at the morning paper until he was seated on the airplane he was taking to the capital of the state. He had a legal-political task there that day.

"Yes, coffee and toast," he told the hostess absently, for he was reading Anne's account of the meeting. It had made the front page and that would delight Anne. It pleased Francis too, and yet there was a little reservation in his satisfaction. Reporting social events was one thing, but writing up this kind of thing—of course she wasn't commenting on it and it was her job. But last night, when she had been telling him about the row, she had sounded a little worked up. She was a brilliant girl, he thought. And she was going to be a wonderful wife, one to be proud of and help a man to get ahead. He wondered—there was a touch of apprehension in the speculation—would Anne be as fertile as her sister? How many children did Joyce have now, five or six? There was no sense in overdoing it—use a little restraint; people had to work these things out and the less said about it the better. Strange that Baird didn't keep his wife from fighting with a lot of old battleaxes about a thing like birth control.

Anne's heart had given a quick leap as she saw the position of her story. It was Saturday and her day off from her job, for the Sunday edition of the women's section was always prepared well in advance of publication. She ran down three flights of stairs, a little earlier than usual, to pick up the newspaper, and unrolled it as she went back to her room at the top of the house. She had two rooms. That was the advantage of renting living quarters in an old-fashioned house which of course had no elevator.

She read her story twice and it stood up well, fast-paced and interesting. Completely factual, too, she assured herself. It was only because of that very large picture of Clare Baird that the impression of her personal defeat was so strong. Anne repeated mentally, that's exactly what happened, that's just how it was. I didn't exaggerate a thing. But she felt a small nagging dissatisfaction in spite of that front-page by-line.

She set about making a breakfast that could be pleasantly leisurely today. Her living quarters were in a kind of turret on a big Victorian house that had been a mansion sixty years before and was now a rooming house. Anne had chosen it with delight. The rent was low enough so she could afford not to have a roommate—she had never been successful with them at college because occasional solitude was one of her necessities. And she did not want what she called the terrible convenience of a one-room utility flat.

From the windows of her round little sitting and sleeping

room she could see the full south slope of the city, and beyond, except in the frozen months, she could watch the merchant boats and the curious foreign ships that continually plowed the seaway. The kitchen, which certainly had once been a trunk room, was gay with bright-colored dishes and trays. Most of them had come from Sears or Woolworth's, but there was also a set of delicate old pink-flowered Haviland china that had belonged to her grandmother.

Anne and her sister, Mary Joyce, had been the charges of their paternal grandmother while they were growing up. Their father, whom Anne could not remember, had been a test pilot in the Army between the world wars. He was killed in one of the accidents which were the constant hazard of his profession—so briefly reported and quickly forgotten by the public. Anne had been born only a few months before the tragedy, in the raw, rather gypsy settlement of Air Force families near the field to which Captain Milner was attached at the time.

There was no place for his widow there. Her own people offered no welcome or refuge, for, as Anne and Joyce figured it out later, remarriages on that side of the family had made it as indifferent as it was distant geographically. From the cold bitterness of their grandmother when the Harrison family was mentioned, and from overheard scraps of conversation, the girls gleaned the fact that Julia Milner's closest relative was a flighty stepmother who wanted no responsibility for her or the children. So the young widow went to the upstate city in New York where her husband's mother had always lived.

She must have insisted on having a place of her own and had enough bonus or insurance money to manage that much independence. Anne could vaguely recall the little house— there was a bush with brilliant-red berries by the front steps and there had to be a dishpan under the place where the roof always leaked in heavy rains. Anne remembered always how she used to pray to the Blessed Virgin to stop the rains before the pan might overflow during the night. Joyce began to take piano lessons in spite of the leak and had made her First Communion before Julia Milner died of a malignant cancer, almost as unexpectedly and swiftly as her husband had gone when the engine of his plane failed.

Anne was five years old and Joyce eleven when their grandmother took them one night to a funeral parlor where a few people were monotonously chanting the rosary for their dead mother. They heard so many people say how hard it was on their grandmother to have to take care of two little girls at her time of life that they were very quiet with apology, and very aware of being burdens. They did not want to leave their little house and go to live in the much larger one that belonged to the elder Mrs. Milner. After the move was made they often crept into each other's bed at night for comfort.

"Of course your mother was a convert," Mrs. Milner told them. She did not say it unkindly, but there was demotion in the statement. She explained, "I don't know what she was before, but she only came into the Church when she married your father. Not having been born a Catholic, she probably thought it was all right to allow you to go to public school when you came here to Syracuse. I have always thoroughly disapproved of it, although of course I didn't say anything."

That unspoken but thorough disapproval may have been one of the reasons why Julia Milner had wanted a home of her own. The girls never saw their mother at the Communion rail. But she sent them to the nearest Catholic church and also to the rather haphazard classes in religious instruction which were provided for public school pupils.

It was different after her death. Their grandmother was a strict Catholic who carried her religion into all phases of her life, even the social ones. People were "our kind" or they were not. She would not have dreamed of disobeying the constant injunction of the priests that Catholic children belonged in Catholic schools. The girls were soon enrolled in

St. Michael's parochial school. Joyce was absorbed more quickly and happily into its pious routine than was Anne.

Putting a pink-flowered Haviland coffee cup on her breakfast tray this morning, Anne for some reason visualized her grandmother. She had been a very handsome woman even in her older years. Her gray hair was firmly curled, her eyes large and clear, her figure rather stately. Yet she had always suggested obedience rather than authority to Anne, in spite of her own ideas and preference. Mrs. Milner never broke even a small rule of the Church. On the kitchen calendar, which was sent once a year to all the parishioners of St. Michael's, the days of fast and abstinence were marked by pictures of fish and the important saints' days by their names and presumable likenesses. Every Sunday and holy day of obligation Mrs. Milner would put the contribution for her share of Church needs into an envelope, and had it ready for the collection basket when it was passed around. Remembering that unbroken sequence of envelopes, Anne felt that her own performance now was very slack. She so often forgot to bring the right envelope to Mass or had only a ten-dollar bill in her purse and did not want to contribute that much. Her memories, now loosed, ran on. She recalled with amusement her grandmother's fascinated interest in the annual reports of parish support, printed with names and amounts.

"I should think they'd be ashamed with that big house and all," she would say, coming upon some name.

But if Joyce or Anne asked with curiosity who it was or how much had been given, Mrs. Milner was sure to reprimand them. "Never you mind. You never know people's circumstances. Remember there's the sin of scandal."

She was a good woman, thought Anne, filling her cup with steaming coffee. But she never could bridge the age gap between herself and us. She didn't really know what we were thinking. Joyce was her favorite. She always said that I took after my mother, and there was a little cutting edge to that.

She would turn over in her grave if she could see the newspaper this morning, with my name connected with a story about birth control. To her that would be an unmentionable thing. She had a tough time with her own family. Grandfather didn't live to be very old, but she had five or six children who were stillborn or died when they were infants—there must have been something really wrong with her physically. My father was the only one of her children who lived and he was killed. She must have suffered, felt terribly bereft. And I wasn't much comfort to her. But Joyce was. She was very proud when the nuns praised Joyce.

In the parochial school Joyce had become devout, and she happily went on to the Convent of the Holy Grove when she graduated from St. Michael's. There she became a Child of Mary and wore the pale-blue ribbon slanting over the shoulder of her uniform, which was a symbol of belonging to that group. She left a tradition of lovely piety and character at the convent, and Anne knew she was expected to carry it on when she was sent there in her turn five years later.

Everybody has always loved Joyce, thought Anne, and carried her tray over to the table by the window. And they should. Chris simply dotes on her. He's never known there was another woman in the world since he first saw her in Syracuse. I wonder if Francis would feel that way about me after eight years. After six children. It's easy to talk about growing potatoes and having goats, but a man never realizes . . . I don't think Chris does, either. I must try to see Joyce today, I'll have lots of time. It's fun to be living in the same city with her. That's why I wanted a job on a newspaper here.

How I missed Joyce, especially before I got away from the convent and into the university. There was a battle with Grandmother over that. Luckily Sister Cleo was on my side. She thought I should go to the university if I wanted journalism, and she didn't believe I'd lose my faith. I can hear her calmly telling Grandmother that. I can see her—big, confident eyes, the white honeycomb ruff around her face and the little mustache that used to fascinate all the girls. I owe a lot to Sister Cleo. After Joyce I was a disappointment to most of the nuns—just an ugly duckling who couldn't learn to play the piano. Then Sister Cleo made me an editor of that smug little magazine they used to misprint and I felt like a big shot. Anne grimaced at the memory of the convent magazine and looked again at her by-line in the newspaper beside her. She grimaced also at her meandering thoughts, put the old memories aside and began to plan her day. With Francis out of town she would have time to catch up on a good many things that had been postponed or neglected.

She washed her hair and shaped it, the front fringe straight and high on her forehead, the sides loosely curved. Golden lights began to come out in it as it dried, and in her blue smock and shorts she looked like a pageboy, surely one of noble blood. She did her housework with affection, making the rooms clean and orderly but not too neat for ease. The fuchsia plant had another blossom, and she thought it might look better on the bookcase than on the windowsill. She studied that aesthetic improvement carefully and was sure she was right. She defrosted the refrigerator, decided at last that she was never going to eat the eclair she had been saving for days and threw it out. At ten o'clock she tried to call Joyce.

The operator said that the telephone was out of order. That probably meant that one of the children had left an extension phone off the hook. It was always happening at the Hawley house. Frustrated, Anne put on a dress and coat and went out to do some shopping. She would try the call again later. Joyce might be able to break away and have lunch with her in town.

She shopped for brown walking shoes and bought red ones. She spent a half hour in a bookshop, culling out the books she didn't want to bother reading, and finally bought a novel that she didn't own and wanted to read again. She window-shopped on the way back to her parking place and wondered why she did not covet diamonds. Again she tried to reach Joyce and failed. So she decided that she would drive out to Bay Park and put that phone back on the hook herself.

It was disappointing to find that her sister was not at home. An unfamiliar baby sitter, who was putting up her hair in enormous curlers, said that Mr. and Mrs. Hawley and the two oldest boys had gone to the football game and were staying in town for dinner. That made the possibility of seeing Joyce today very remote, for the ball park was twenty miles distant from Anne's apartment, and traffic after the game would make driving slow and difficult. But, disappointed in one way, Anne was very glad that Joyce was having a half-day vacation from the care of her whole family.

The baby was in her crib, but Kip and Betty and Sam swarmed about Anne, hoping for presents and finding them, for she had stopped at a supermarket for balloons and pop-corn. With them at her heels she discovered that the extension in the kitchen was the one that was disconnected. They listened with delighted excitement as she told how vainly she had tried to call their mother, and the youngest one immediately tried to pull the phone off the hook again. He was the child who worried Joyce. Kip and Betty were sturdy, beautiful children, and so were the older boys, John and Matthew. But Sam had been premature and had never caught up. He looked fragile and often exhausted as he trailed after the others and tried to match their energies.

The Hawley house was long and rambling and looked as if it had never been completely finished. A couple of bedrooms added on to one end of the original structure, as the number of children increased, had stretched its length but spoiled its shape. In the beginning Joyce had planned carefully and happily. The front room was to be a living room for adults, and the family room on the opposite side of the house would be the playroom for the use of the children. But the family room had long since overflowed into the potential front parlor and now every room in the house was at the mercy of the children.

Anne picked up the baby, who smelled clean and sweet. The baby sitter evidently knew that part of her job, in spite of the curlers. Joyce would have made sure of that. But the job was strictly limited and obviously included no house-keeping. The baby was tiny; she had only weighed four and a half pounds when she was born. Anne glanced down at the little bare left foot. The doctors hoped that it would straighten out. It was too soon to tell.

She put the baby down gently, and while she played with the other children for a couple of hours Anne managed to create some order. She plumped cushions, and matched the stray tennis shoes and abandoned socks that were strewn everywhere, and made a game of filling a wastebasket with Sam's innumerable tin automobiles, and washed smeared door-knobs as well as the dishes that had been left in the sink after the children's lunch. She made sandwiches for their supper and left them in the refrigerator, and also chopped up a bowl of fruit, for the baby sitter did not seem to be in-terested in any kitchen work. It was late afternoon when she drove back to the city.

Francis would not be back in town until nearly midnight. She would have no date tonight and so it would be a good time— She drove slowly, not quite decided about what she half intended to do. It had been in her mind all day. She was thinking of going to confession. But did she want to? Was it necessary? The rules of the Church had been greatly relaxed since her days at St. Michael's school, and confession was no longer required before going to Communion unless a person was in a state of mortal sin. And I'm not, Anne said to herself.

The things that made sin mortal repeated themselves in her mind. The sin had to be grave—that was the first thing. It had to be an action which was a serious breach of the Commandments or the laws of the Church. Also, the sinner had to be conscious of what he was doing and had to do it deliberately. It must be an act of free will. Francis had once said that it took a good lawyer for the prosecution to convince himself of mortal sin.

But I don't feel . . . worthy, she thought. When she was a child, she had almost held her breath from the time the priest absolved her until she received the Host at an early Mass, trying to keep absolutely sinless in the meantime. She thought, I haven't been to confession for more than a month and I've gone to Communion every Sunday. There have been so many little meannesses—and impulses, even if I didn't let them go too far. I don't feel that I have a right to keep on receiving Communion without going to confession. For another thing, I'm too uncertain, I have too many doubts.

The cathedral loomed up across the square. She had been driving toward it. She argued with herself, if I don't do it now I'd be resisting grace. She parked the car and entered the shadowy church. It was very silent. Not a whisper could be heard though there were perhaps more than thirty people to be seen, some kneeling in the pews, some lined up against the wall near one of the confessionals, waiting their turn. The longest line was outside the box over which Father Jerrold's name could be read. He was known never to be harsh.

Anne had never chosen one priest to be her confessor. She preferred complete anonymity when she sought the Sacrament of Penance, not knowing who heard what she told and knowing that to the listening priest she was only a voice and a soul. There was almost always a visiting priest hearing confessions in the huge cathedral parish, and he would be in the front box, where there was a small light to indicate occupancy but no name above the door. In a pew close to that one Anne went to her knees and searched her mind before she entered the confessional.

"Bless me, Father, for I have sinned."

The voice blessed her.

"Father, I went to confession six weeks ago and since then I have gone to Communion every Sunday." The routine imbedded in her mind in childhood was smooth and familiar at first: ". . . careless and neglectful of my prayers . . . sins of unkindness . . ." She paused.

"Yes—is there more?"

This she always had hated—were there sins of impurity? Where did one draw the line? What did she have to confess? The agony of the two times she had confessed childish unchastity could come back with nausea—not today.

"With men—one man—I've been sometimes not quite modest —gone farther than I intended. It wasn't anything wrong—"

"Are you a married woman?"

"No, Father."

"These occasions of immodesty—did they produce orgasm?"

"No, Father."

"You must avoid the occasion of sin, my child. One can slip almost unwittingly into habits which become . . ."

She thought of Francis, wondering if he confessed how he sometimes held her, and brought her attention back to the homily.

"You have committed no mortal sin? Of that you are sure?"

"Only venial ones, Father. But they pile up—they accumulate until sometimes you don't feel as if you should receive Communion."

"Grace brings you to the Sacrament of Penance. Is there anything else?"

"No, Father, only perhaps—there is one thing that bothers me. . . ."

"Yes?"

"It's about birth control, Father. I can't help feeling that the people who believe in it are good people and—well, the ones who have studied about the population explosion and explored the situation feel that it's necessary. I sometimes feel that the stand of the Church is behind the times. . . ."

"The natural law will never be behind the times," said the

priest. "The doctrine of the Church in regard to contraception is based on the fact that it is a violation of the natural law. When a person employs a human faculty in an unnatural manner, perverting its natural object, he is disobeying the natural law, which is nothing else than the law of God. And God is never behind the times. For all time is His."

His voice was kind, firm, sure. Anne was silent.

"You say you are not a married woman?"

"No, Father."

"Have you ever been married?"

"No."

"May I ask your age?"

"I am twenty-five."

"Are you betrothed?"

What a lovely word, Anne thought irrelevantly.

"Not exactly. But I think I shall marry a certain man I know some day."

"Is he a Catholic?"

"Yes, he is."

"Ah," said the priest with satisfaction, "then before you marry, my dear child, you and this man must face what marriage involves, what it demands. And bestows. The Church does not seek to regulate the number of children you may have. There is considerable misunderstanding in regard to that. But it commands you not to violate the natural law, for that is mortal sin. Before you marry, you should discuss these things with your parish priest, who will explain to you that a man and a woman, not the officiating priest, are the ministers of the Sacrament of Matrimony. Now, is there anything else?"

"No, Father."

"For your penance say ten Our Fathers and ten Hail Marys in honor of the Blessed Mother. Make a good Act of Contrition."

Chapter 3

∿∿∿

Christopher had fallen asleep almost immediately, but Joyce could not. For a little while she lay still, happily exhausted with love-making, and then the question which she had first ignored and then forgotten during the last hour rose in her mind. When it became apprehension, she slipped noiselessly from her bed and crossed the room to the dressing table, feeling among the other things on top of it for a little framed calendar that always stood there. She did not turn on any light for fear of waking Chris in the adjoining bed, but there was always a night light in the hall in case one of the children should begin to ramble around the house.

She stood close to the ray of light, a beautiful, rumpled ghost, with dark hair tossed back and a pale-blue nightgown slipping from one perfectly molded shoulder, studying the dates and counting again. Yes, it had been that Thursday last time, which meant that tonight was on the far edge of the safe period. But of course sometimes a day or two made no difference. Not with most women, but it can with me, she thought. It was that way with the baby. I was pretty sure that time and look—though of course I couldn't be more glad about her.

It was my fault tonight as much as his, she told herself. If

I'd been firm tonight with Chris, he'd have gone off to sleep. But it was such a good day and he'd had such fun at the game—he doesn't have a chance to have that much relaxation very often—I didn't want to spoil the day arguing about whether we should or not. And of course it was partly the bourbon. He'd already had a drink with that friend he met at the ball park during the intermission, and then when we got to the restaurant he had three more. I'm a fine one, too. If I hadn't had two whisky sours, I might have had more sense tonight. When you feel just a little high it doesn't seem so much of a chance.

She had a drink of water in the bathroom, quietly put the calendar back where it belonged and felt completely awake. Disastrously awake, for she needed to sleep tonight. Sunday was always the busiest and most crowded day in the week. The four older children had to be decently dressed for church instead of pulling on the nearest pair of blue jeans. And Chris was home all day and dinner was at two in the afternoon—it was a leg of lamb tomorrow. And that will take at least two hours and a half in the oven; it's a big one. She planned: I'll let Chris sleep late and not wake him until just before I go to the ten o'clock Mass. The baby usually sleeps through after she's fed, and Chris can get his own breakfast and take the boys to the eleven o'clock. He won't want to go to Communion, but I do. I'll have coffee and a piece of toast at seven and that will be a full three hours' fast.

I might start a novena. No, not for that. It would be almost sacrilegious to start a novena not to have another baby. But, dear God, where would we put another one? This house is bursting at the seams now and besides—after what the doctor told me, how could I face him?

She recalled Dr. Helm's gravity. It was when they had last discussed the baby's foot and that breathlessness of Sam's. Dr. Helm had asked her again how old she was. Thirty then—thirty-one now. And he had said, "Six children in eight years. That's quite a family, Joyce."

"It's what you marry for," she had said and laughed.

"Other reasons for matrimony have been alleged," he remarked in his dry way.

"Of course. I didn't mean that it was the only one."

She was devoted to Dr. Helm. She trusted him completely. Always, when she came out of the anesthetic, he was there, destroying the pain and making the world safe. He was the best gynecologist in the city. And Dr. Helm was fond of her, she knew that too.

"You're a good girl, Joyce. You're a good woman."

"Not so very. You don't know the half of it, Doctor."

"But none the less I think you'll have to go slow now—very slow. These children need you."

"I will. I always snap back after the first few weeks."

"I'm not thinking so much of you as of the children."

She had asked, "What do you mean about them?"

"Well, you've had four splendid kids. But the last two didn't come out quite so well. Sam doesn't seem to have the pep of the others, does he?"

"He's not quite so strong."

"Maybe because you didn't have so much to give when you were carrying him. You've had them too fast, Joyce. That may be why this infant isn't quite . . . complete."

"You think the foot will grow and straighten out, though. That's what you said."

"That's what I said I hoped."

"Oh . . ."

"We'll hope for the best. And it wouldn't be too bad a handicap even if she didn't overcome it."

"She'd be lame. Always?"

"Presumably. Just don't expect too much."

"And Sam? He's really all right, isn't he?"

"We'll keep an eye on Sam. Don't let him overstrain himself."

"He tries so hard to keep up with the others."

"He can't do it," said the doctor. "He's more nervous than

those other titans of yours. You are going to have your hands full for the next ten or fifteen years taking care of this family."

"I know, but I adore it."

The doctor had said bluntly, "I think you and Chris should call it a day now."

"You mean not have any more children?"

"That's what I mean exactly."

"Well, Doctor," she said, "that's what we really think too. Because we have to educate them. And that's getting to be so terribly expensive. Chris and I have talked it over. We feel that we have a large enough family—just what you think."

"I seem to remember that you told me that before this last little codger came along."

"I know, Doctor," Joyce had said, flushing, "but it just happened. We did try to be so careful. I watched the dates like anything. I couldn't have been more surprised. Not that I'm not terribly glad and grateful to have my baby. But we just couldn't figure how it could happen."

"It can happen all right. The rhythm method isn't reliable. It works all right in some cases. But you're a remarkably fertile woman."

"I guess I must be. Poor Chris. But what can I do?"

"You could be fitted."

She said slowly, "I wouldn't want that."

"And if you wanted to make perfectly sure, you could have a simple operation. Tie off the Fallopian tubes."

"It's not allowed."

"It's permitted in any first-class hospital on the recommendation of two reliable physicians. I could arrange for a second one. It's constantly done and quite safe. Mind you, I wouldn't recommend it or perform the operation for a woman who didn't want children for any selfish reason. Because they might interfere with her trips to Europe or her bridge tournaments or because she'd rather have a mink coat than pay for a baby. But that's not your case. You've had six children, an average of one a year. You evidently can't continue at that rate—you'll play yourself out and be a less useful mother, and also, and even more important, your last children are not keeping up to the physical standards of the first ones you had. For you I'd not only okay the operation if you want it but I'd be willing to perform it."

"That would mean I couldn't have any more children at all, ever?"

"That's right."

"The Church wouldn't allow me to have that done."

He said, "Well, I've performed the operation for a number of Catholic women. For reasons of their health—sometimes their incompetency. I don't know too much about their status in your Church subsequently, but from what I've heard I believe a *fait accompli* is usually accepted. Your Church is liberal in forgiveness."

He had said that last with a slight cynicism and then more kindly, "Would you like me to talk with Chris about this?"

"No, please. I'd rather you didn't, Doctor. He's working hard and I don't want him to feel worried. Doctor, does that operation make any difference to a man?"

"In pleasure in sex relations? Not at all. To neither a man or a woman. In fact, it often improves those relations because the fear of consequences which they don't want is removed."

"I see. Don't talk to Chris, Doctor Helm. I will, and I'll be terribly careful from now on."

She decided to talk to her confessor before she spoke to Chris. And after she heard what the priest said, she had not brought up the matter of the operation with her husband. For the priest had been inflexible.

"You would commit a mortal sin. You would repent that sin for the rest of your life. Even if you were readmitted to the Sacraments, you would still have to face God in final judgment with that sin on your soul. And who knows what His punishment might be? Not only in eternity but in your temporal life? If one or more of your children met with accident or death—and sometimes many in one family or even whole families are wiped out in a single disaster—you could not turn to God and ask Him to give you another child to comfort you.

"Now, the Church does not ask you to increase your family. You have six children and so you have been blessed by God six times—He has created six souls and trusted you with them. Are you so ungrateful for these blessings that you will arrogantly disobey His law? You tell me that your physician has advised you against further pregnancy. You may tell him that you will take his advice and that you and your husband will practice abstinence. And that it is also within the law of God for you to have relations with your husband at times when it is improbable that you will conceive."

What had most shaken Joyce was that accusation of ingratitude. When she saw the health and gaiety of her children, as she watched the baby reach and learn to creep and try to talk, she would think, suppose I did have that operation and anything happened to one of them?

But there were times when fatigue made a wave of self-pity sweep over her, when the children's demands seemed as mischievous as their breakage and when Christopher's acceptance of her multiple tasks infuriated her. Then she would imagine what it might be like to be sure that this confusion would never get worse, that she could plan ahead with certainty that when she was utterly tired she could creep into Christopher's bed and fall asleep in his arms without the worry, without the knowledge that she would have to wait three or four weeks before she could be sure that she wasn't pregnant again.

She was back in her bed now, watching a pattern of shadows move against the white wall of the bedroom. There was a moon tonight and a restless wind. The shadows of the leaves seemed helplessly wild and undirected. She thought, sometimes you can't help it. You can tell yourself that it's the wrong time, that you simply must not take a chance. And then the feeling grows, then finally you don't care—nothing is so important as the climax, with me the same as with him. I wonder if I'm more passionate than most women. It's probably all right tonight. I think I'm safe enough. She slept at last and the pattern of the leaves moved over the wall until it was on her pillow like a wreath.

Chapter 4

∾∾∾

The city editor of the *Observer*, Max Fleming, never wasted his time in praising any member of his staff. Sometimes it seemed that he hardly identified them personally, and then suddenly he would single someone out for a special job. The constantly growing circulation of the newspaper was due to Fleming's instinct for knowing what people would like to read before they were aware of it themselves. There was not a world or national event that escaped his notice, and he related each one to the interests and values in his own region with unerring precision.

He said to Anne Milner, whom he had called into his office, "This county commissioner's fight over reliefers—you been following it, Anne?"

"More or less. You mean the row that man Porada started? I didn't know how much of it was politics."

"Porada's trying to get publicity for himself, of course, so he'll be re-elected commissioner. But this stink he's raising about women having kids so they can collect more money on relief may have something in it. Seems to be happening in a good many places over the country. I'd like to have a feature story on it. I was going to turn it over to Bill Plaunt, but I have an idea that you might get farther with some of these women. They might talk more freely with you than with Bill. Think so?"

"I'd certainly like to dig into that."

"Not a sob story," said Fleming, "a good, hard piece of news is what I want out of this. Is the tax money being used to populate the county with a lot of brats that nobody wants? Are desertions framed up so the women can collect relief? How do the kids live? What's their future? How many are bastards? No actual names, of course, but actual facts. I'd use it in the Sunday Cosmo section if it works out. You'll have to bone up on the general situation, but only for background. What our readers want to know isn't what's happening in Boston but what's going on right here under their noses."

"Yes, of course. I'll read up on it in the library—there have been a lot of articles in the magazines—and then I'll know what to look for in the local situation."

"Talk to Porada, of course. He claims to know actual cases and he'll be tickled to have his attack played up."

Fleming hitched his glasses to the top of his bald head. He was conscious of Anne's excitement at the assignment and pleased with it. But he went on to warn her.

"The paper wouldn't want to take a stand, even if a lot of hocus-pocus is going on. Interfering with sex life, even with paupers and criminals, is very tricky business. Controversial as hell. But you could slant the piece so there would be plenty of argument. Quote opinions—other people's ideas. Such as some people think—that in the interest of lower taxes and relieving the load on our public institutions the country should pass out birth control pills along with relief checks and groceries." He grinned at Anne and added, "Maybe you could get a statement on that from Mrs. Angus Baird."

"I could always try," said Anne with equal irony.

"She certainly got herself into a peck of trouble."

"I don't think she really expected those clubwomen to back her up."

"That's the least of it. The story is going around that the sales of the Baird Company are falling off because of what she's been doing. That the Catholics are boycotting Baird products. You ought to know if that's true. You're a Catholic, aren't you?"

"Yes, I am, but I'm sure . . ."

She did not finish what she had started to say and Fleming did not press her. He always avoided talk of religion if possible. He said abruptly, "Well, see what you can turn out on this relief business—take a week or ten days if you need it."

Anne left the office and went back to her own desk. She had been delighted with the prospect of doing a feature article, but for the moment what Fleming had said about the Baird Company was on the top of her thoughts. She had been about to tell him that a Catholic boycott was absurd and impossible, and then all at once she had remembered that sermon in the cathedral two weeks ago.

That disastrous sermon. It had prevented her from receiving Communion. Father Collins was often a scolding priest, but he had been more vehement than usual in his diatribes against sin in married life. Anne recalled the substance of some of his statements. "Catholics are engaged in a holy war against all those who publicly or privately advocate the artificial prevention of birth." I couldn't go along with that and I still can't, Anne said to herself now. Just because people have a different point of view doesn't bring on a holy war. And then he ranted on about not giving economic support or sentimental sympathy to our enemies. Economic support—did he mean boycott? I didn't think of that at the time. But he was so violent and exaggerated that I began to think that Clare Baird made more sense than he did. And wonder if I was going to let my married life be dominated by Father Collins. By the time he finished I certainly wasn't in a state of grace. It wasn't mortal sin, but I couldn't go up to the altar rail feeling so critical and rebellious.

Nor had she received Communion on this last Sunday. But I will next week, she promised herself. I'll go to one of the very early Masses, when Father Collins will not preach. The resolve felt satisfying and Anne turned her thoughts to her new assignment. Obviously the first thing to do was to talk to Mr. Porada. With luck she might even be able to make an appointment with him for this afternoon.

Carl Porada had been quite willing to see her, and it had been so easy to contact him and fix the time for an interview that the city editor's skepticism about Porada's motive in declaring that there was corruption on the relief rolls was also in Anne's mind when she sought him out in his room at the county courthouse at four o'clock. She could not recall having seen a picture of this commissioner who had not been long in office. The courthouse was not her usual beat. But she expected to meet a beefy politician with an oratorical manner who would talk platitudes for publicity purposes, and Porada's appearance surprised her as much as his attitude.

He was quite young and completely unlike the mental picture she had conjured up. Carl Porada was certainly in his early thirties, a thin young man, not very neat or well pressed, and he was not in the least assertive. He stood up when she came in, did not shake hands, motioned her to a chair across from where he himself sat and looked at her over a confusion of papers strewn on his desk. Then he asked, "What do you want to see me about?"

She explained her assignment. She overexplained it, because he was so silent and unresponsive. He listened without looking at her, and as she finished and he did not say anything Anne felt she had not made any impression.

She said, "I believe you told the commissioners that you know actual cases in which relief has almost become a way of life."

"Leave out that 'almost,'" said Porada.

"I'd be very glad to."

"Why?"

"It's always a better story without any almosts," she said.

He did look at her now and not with approval.

But she went on with it. "I'd like to explore some of those cases, Mr. Porada. Talk to some of the people involved. Especially those women who you said were making illegitimate childbearing a career. Is that a correct quotation?"

"Correct enough."

"And it was reported in the paper that you said that sometimes two generations of a family were living on relief. If you would give me the names of some such people—"

"We don't give out the names of our clients for such purposes," he said shortly.

"I wouldn't use the real names, Mr. Porada. Just facts. But to get their point of view I have to talk to the women."

"What good would that do?"

"Well, what I want—what I would try to do is to give the public a picture of the kind of people who exploit relief. And what their excuse is, if they have any. It's a way of making this more real to the public so any corruption can be stopped and—"

Carl Porada interrupted her. "Listen Miss—sorry, your name escapes me."

"Anne Milner."

"Miss Milner, I'm not trying to punish anyone. Or make it harder for these people. They don't have it very good, you know."

"But you said that they are getting money under false pretenses."

"Sure they are. A woman will say her husband has deserted her and apply for aid for her dependent children. The government ponies up—we are committed to match the amount. Maybe the husband is living across the street and visiting her nights. Or maybe someone who isn't her husband will be the father of her third bastard. That bastard is worth $23.10 a month to her. She's an adept liar, and often she's lived on relief so long that she knows every trick in the bag. But I don't want to parade the poor creature through the streets in your newspaper or anywhere else."

"Then why did you start anything? After all, Mr. Porada, you're the one who broke this wide open in a meeting of the commissioners and before the press. I'm just following it up."

"That's right, I started it," he said, "and I'll tell you why. First, because of the money. The load is getting too heavy for the traffic to bear in this county. There's a lot of tax delinquency. We can't afford to carry people on the relief rolls if they might be earning."

"Could most of them be earning?"

"Some of them. If they haven't forgotten how. But let me finish. That's one reason, the one that gets under the taxpayer's skin. But there's a more important reason. Most of these kids shouldn't be born. They shouldn't be allowed to come into the world, even if there is a kind of bounty paid for them. Because they don't have a chance. They see things that kids shouldn't see going on in the places where they have to live. They rot when they're just kids. They get beaten up. The little girls are violated." He stopped and stared at Anne, who met his eyes with her own straightforward glance.

"Then you think the answer is that the children shouldn't be born?"

"Not unless they are wanted for a better reason than the money every dependent child brings in."

"You approve of sterilization, Mr. Porada?"

He hesitated, made a face of distaste. "The idea sort of gags me. These people are helpless, they're at the mercy of the government. And it never could be put over anyway. Wherever that proposition has been suggested, it's been beaten to a pulp. But these birth control people might get busy in their own bailiwick instead of worrying about the population explosion in India."

Max Fleming would like that remark for a lead, thought Anne. But she was afraid to ask if she might quote the commissioner. It was more important to persuade him to give her the names of people she could interview.

"Maybe they do try," she said.

"Of course they have to fight the priests," said Porada, "who want more souls for God." He checked himself, then suddenly grinned at Anne, and she felt an attractive—and disarming—recklessness in this grim young man. He said, "I'm getting my neck out pretty far. May I request that you don't quote me?"

"I won't. I didn't come to interview you, Mr. Porada, but to ask for help. I can go to the relief rolls myself—they're open to the public—and investigate on my own. But it would save a whole lot of time and probably be much more accurate if I could get some direction from you. I don't want to sound personal, but I'm terribly interested—and not just because I want a story. I think this is something I should know about, even if I weren't on a newspaper."

"I thought you were in earnest when you telephoned. Or I wouldn't have been so available. I don't know why, but I expected a social-worker type, an older woman, and when you came in, you sort of threw me. Well, I tell you what I'll do." His hands moved swiftly among the disorderly papers and extracted a document.

"This is the data from our workers in the field, which I used when I was putting together that statement for the Board of Commissioners. It has names and addresses and facts. You can look it over and choose what you want to follow up. But you'll have to do it here and now. I don't want this to go out of the office. And I'll have to leave you with it, for I have a meeting."

54

"I am so grateful, Mr. Porada."

"Okay," he said and turned from the doorway to give her a surprisingly friendly wink, "but no names—no identification of clients that can embarrass them—and no quotes of Carl Porada. That's the bargain?"

"That's the bargain!"

"Don't spare the horses—try to start the public thinking," he said and went rapidly down the hall.

Chapter 5

❧❧❧

The atmosphere of the meeting was unusually formal and almost uncomfortable. Most of the directors did not know whether the subject would be introduced for frank discussion or dealt with in some roundabout way, without mentioning the name of the president's wife. But in many conversations during the past fortnight it had been agreed that the drop in sales could not be overlooked, no matter how much Angus Baird might be embarrassed.

It came into the open in the proper place, after the usual report on the condition of their business. A mimeographed sheet before each director showed that in September of the previous year sales had been almost nine per cent higher. They studied the figures, some with no change of expression, some with a frown, as Charley Sanders, the sales manager, talked. These were men who were not only successful but accustomed to improving on success. That was why they were members of this Board.

"Have you some explanation for the way sales have been falling off recently, Mr. Sanders?" That was Mr. Ginn, making a courteous inquiry to begin with.

Charley Sanders looked down at the figures as if to be sure he had not missed some significance. He said, "To some extent,

I think, it reflects the current uncertainty of business. Retail sales are generally down—everyone is waiting to see if there is going to be a tax cut and how big it will be if one comes. In the meantime the consumer is going slow or actually re-trenching."

"From what I see in the financial journals retail sales in most instances are down less than one per cent."

"That's correct, Mr. Ginn."

"It doesn't seem to me that our products, especially baby foods, are subject to whimsical buying," said Clyde Ferris. "They would probably be one of the last items on which the housewife would retrench."

Now we are off, thought Herbert Martin. The fat's in the fire. With the supersensitiveness to human relations which was his special talent and earned him his living he knew that the roots of feeling about the matter coming to the surface would be bedded deep in temperament and conviction. Possibly in prejudice. Martin sat as usual at the far end of the table from Angus Baird's place, and his chair was pushed back a little farther than those in which the others sat. He was a consultant, not a director, though he often attended these meetings.

He had a considered opinion about each man. Clyde Ferris was a mean-spirited fellow, but valuable because he was so quick to understand any factor which might be advantageous. Funston Smith had to have things carefully explained, and he didn't always catch on to undertones or overtones. But he was tenaciously rich and so a good deterrent to any suggestion of plunging. His basic principle, as he himself expressed it, was "My father left me a little money and I mean to hang on to it."

Kingsley Jones had long been hypnotized by the spread of his name and influence. His name was on the letterhead of dozens of philanthropic and improve-the-world projects. Was he a sponsor of Planned Parenthood, Martin wondered? There was Solomon Frank, the only Jew on the Board, as he was the only Jew in so many highly respected places, including the very exclusive Old Town Club.

Morrow was a Catholic—but perhaps only a nominal one. He was very social and married to a Clark. The Clarks were a worldly, globe-trotting family. But Mr. Ginn's wife was a devout Catholic. Everyone knew that she had given the magnificent stained-glass windows made in Belgium to the cathedral, as well as the chimes which rang out melodiously three times a day over that section of the city, though few of the residents observed the devotion of the Angelus.

The only sure thing about Peter Daniels was that he was not predictable. Daniels had come up the hard way and by this time it was a very long way. Possibly, Martin had figured, he was not quite at ease with men who had inherited fortunes. Sometimes he would sit through an entire meeting of the directors without opening his mouth except to cast a gruff vote one way or another. But if he did suggest something, he would follow through on it. Paul Redfern and young Allen were both fairly new on the Board. They would probably wait to see which way the cat would jump if there was any argument.

It's very tricky, thought Martin. No one will want to attack the Catholics or run them down though they all have been talking privately about a Catholic boycott. And that in itself is difficult to prove. It's hard to pinpoint just what is being done. The Roman Catholic Church is so well organized that it can be very subtle and accomplish its purposes without openly declaring or publishing them. It can use its traditional methods over individuals—the hold of their clergy over birth and death—and this time it's marriage. There are hundreds of church societies where the word can be passed around quietly. There isn't a priest or bishop at this table, Martin said to himself, but what they may have advised or enjoined is right here with us.

"At this rate," said Ferris, "we might have to pass the December dividend."

Funston Smith owned three thousand shares. As he mentally multiplied by fifteen he exclaimed querulously, "That would be outrageous. We haven't passed a dividend since 1932."

"Maybe something is the matter with our sales force, Mr. Sanders. Have they lost their momentum, or their pep?"

"It's not that, sir. To be frank, they've—so they tell me, and they're disturbed as much as we are—they've run up against rather widespread criticism."

"Of our baby foods?" Clyde Ferris was pushing, forcing the issue. He didn't care whether there was a row or not.

"No, it's not criticism of our products," said Angus Baird. "Charley is referring to my wife's participation in the planned-parenthood movement."

There was as dead a silence as if someone had suggested a moment of prayer. Why did Clare let herself in for this, Martin thought in angry frustration. Why did she have to go looking for trouble? She and Angus had everything. Angus can be obtuse, but he's always been mad for her, never looked at another woman. He would have tried to give her the moon if she'd asked for it. If giving her the moon wouldn't hurt the corporation. And she was in love with him from the word go. No one else ever had a chance with her, thought Herbert Martin, who had not married because he had never met a woman who could give him what Angus Baird had taken. Even friendship and the occasional sight or presence of Clare had dulled Martin's desire for anyone else.

"How extraordinary," said Funston Smith as the moment dragged on too long. He spoke as if this were news to him, as it certainly was not. He asked, "Do you believe there's anything to that, Angus?"

"I wasn't inclined to," said Baird quietly. "It seemed rather absurd. But I've been forced to believe that there is a cause-and-effect relation between my wife's activities in this movement and our sales. Herb brought it to my attention in the first place, and since then Charley has done some pretty thorough investigating. Evidently a certain amount of antagonism on this account exists. I regret this very much."

Now that his name had been mentioned, Herbert Martin knew that it was his turn.

He said, "Mrs. Baird, for various reasons, was given an unusual amount of publicity in connection with her assumption of the state presidency of the birth control organization. Anything relating to what is called the population explosion attracts attention right now, and the national news magazines carried stories about Mrs. Baird's interest in it. Often there was mention that Mrs. Baird was the wife of the president of the Baird Baby Food company. There was also a clubwomen's action locally which excited some feeling, and the Associated Press unfortunately picked that up and featured it out of all proportion to its importance."

"Yes, I read about the clubwomen's fight," said someone with a chuckle.

Mr. Ginn spoke. "I don't think it can be dismissed lightly," he began. "This is a distasteful subject which properly should be kept within the confines of individual families and their personal advisers. But the discussion of it has been brought into open forums and is bandied about in the press. The ones responsible for this are not quiet, orderly people, minding their own business, but apparently a group who seem to feel they have a right to impose their opinions about the most delicate matters of family life on others, including those whose religion and training oppose the doctrines of the so-called planners of parenthood. To me the whole business is unpleasant, even repugnant, one more evidence of deteriorating standards in American life. But I can understand the point of view—and the values—of those elements in our society who feel that they must protest and contest this"—he repeated the word with emphasis—"deterioration."

"Now," he went on, and they were all listening closely, a medley of expressions on the faces around the table, "we are, we members of this Board, to some extent a family, with common interests. Also in our family are many thousands of workers who are not privileged to be present at this meeting, but whose interests are identical with ours, those interests being the manufacturing and merchandising of food for children and thereby earning our . . . wherewithal. Loyalty to these others is involved. Therefore I think it would not be out of order to request with all respect that any member of our business family, including those close to us who are officers, consider the common interests and act accordingly in regard to actions and affiliations."

It was rebuke, admonition and direction for Clare Baird. But as Mr. Ginn leaned stiffly back in his chair, Solomon Frank's long, spare body moved forward.

He spoke with complete lack of pompousness, almost gently.

"I interpret what you have said, Mr. Ginn, to amount to a request from the directors that Mrs. Baird disassociate herself from the work of planned parenthood. I would consider that to be a yielding to blackmail on the part of the gentlemen around this table. I could not go along with it."

Kingston Jones said, "I would like to offer a word from my own experience, if I may. I have always considered it my duty to help organizations functioning for the public good. I have sponsored many of them. Too many, for my own time and energy, but I never turn down a good cause. When the planned-parenthood group was organized in this state, some of its backers came to me and said, 'Mr. Jones, we want to use your name. We need your name on the letterhead.' I gave the matter consideration—I have friends in the movement and they are people of conscience and good will—but I was also deeply aware that a name, perhaps comparatively well known, loses some dignity when it is attached to controversy, and may do harm to other responsibilities which the owner of the name has assumed. I've never allowed my name to be used politically for that reason. Well, gentlemen, to be brief, I told the ones who came to me in behalf of the birth control movement that, in consideration of my personal and business interests, I could not let them use my name."

"Pretty smart," said Ferris. "Glad you didn't or we might have had a boycott wished on us before now."

No, thought Herbert Martin, it wouldn't have made any difference what Jones did. Nobody would have cared. Probably nobody would have noticed, for Jones would have been only a name. But Clare is a person. It's her fervor for the thing, it's because she means it. . . .

Surprisingly young Paul Redfern was speaking up.

"I feel pretty much as Mr. Frank does," he said. "I gather that the Catholics are ganging up on us because some of us don't see things their way. That's not the way I like to see a game played. And for my money, the majority of people are very much worried about this population thing, and the fact that we may have to make baby foods out of sea water for the next generation."

Everyone except Mr. Ginn laughed and that helped. Redfern asked, "If it's not out of turn, I'd like to ask the chairman if Mrs. Baird is aware that we seem to be up against a boycott that is cutting into our profits pretty deeply?"

Baird said, "I've talked it over with my wife. She—she's deeply interested in the work she's been doing. She'd be very reluctant to give it up. But she is not aware of the actual sales figures—I wasn't myself until Charley came up with them today. I shall certainly tell her about them and also about the concern of the members of the Board."

But it won't make her resign, thought Herbert Martin. And God knows what is going to happen between her and you if she won't. You've talked to her, I've talked to her. Both of you are suffering over this. It's changing you. If you'd found

Clare with another man, you could hardly have been more bitter.

Peter Daniels was growling in the uncultivated voice that was so different from those of the other men, "Can't do anything but coast along on this. Angus is going to talk to his lady, who I happen to admire very much, whether she pulls out of this thing or not. I was one of twelve kids myself and it would have been a hell of a lot better if women had known some of the things then that they are finding out now. Maybe it's like Ginn says, deterio—or whatever—he says we're slipping. Maybe not. I'm not a professor or a priest and I wouldn't know. But I do know one thing." He was hunched over the sales report and he banged one big hand down on it. "Our sales have fallen off. In any business I've ever been working on, when you lose a market or start to take a loss in one, you better hustle and find a new one. Maybe we better stop shouting down the well and put our mind on that."

It was the only time that Martin could remember that Mr. Ginn had been spoken of in that unprefixed way. Nobody smiled, though he was sure that many of the directors were suppressing laughter. But if the elder man wanted to retaliate or repeat his argument, he was blocked. For Solomon Frank, master of both tact and finance, said swiftly, "Quite so. Have you any suggestions as to new markets that we ought to explore, Pete?"

"I been studying over our reports," answered Daniels, "what we're doing outside the USA. We're pretty well set in Australia and New Zealand, and they've slammed the door on us in Europe for the time being. But I don't think we've even scratched the surface in South America. Sure we have a little office in Rio and we buy a few vitamins and have a few outlets in Brazil and Argentina. But that's a big continent and we're only working one side of it. We're not doing anything in Colombia and Ecuador, full of hungry Indian kids. And there's Chile—should be a market. I went around to most of the ports down there once and I never been able to get over what the Singer people did. Planted a sewing machine in every hut and that was twenty-five years ago. I knew another fellow—he went down there in the twenties with a lot of plumbing fixtures. Came back a millionaire."

Angus Baird said, "What do you think, Charley? Are we missing a bet in South America?"

"I've always wanted to promote that," said the sales manager, "but we've had our hands pretty full and expansion takes a lot of capital. It would mean branch plants down there. Shipping finished products is far too expensive."

"We've found that out."

"Also," said Herbert Martin, "it's not just a matter of getting a few acres of land and building a plant. Anything that involves manufacture by a foreign firm is permissive in any South American country. It has to be arranged with the national government and the governments always retain some share of control."

"The oil and steel companies have found ways to deal with them and make money."

"Oh yes, it can be done," said Martin, "if it's found to be advisable."

"There are two things that seem to make it worth exploring," said Solomon Frank. "Everyone knows that the people in those countries want more food and that the growth of population is tremendous. We should have—may I say—a waiting public for our baby foods."

"How about sending down a representative to look around and bring back a report?"

"How about sending Herb?"

Herbert Martin said, "I think it would be a waste of time. You see, we already have most of the basic facts in our files. Where manufacture is advisable, traffic conditions and so forth. We know all about population centers. If anybody goes down, it should be top-flight. The oil and steel corporations continually send down their highest executives. That flatters the national governments and something gets accomplished. Our chairman is the one who should go down there if we want to start something."

And after he spoke he thought of a side benefit. It would be a very good thing for Angus to get away right now. He was brooding over the rift between Clare and himself, and a new project would take his mind off that. Martin was very grateful to Peter Daniels. Thanks to him, the subject of birth control would be sidestepped for the rest of this meeting. As for Clare, when she was confronted with those figures, she would surely wash that organization out of her hair and in time the thing would blow over.

It was true that Angus Baird had been brooding. He still was as he drove toward his home in the early evening. The discussion had angered and humiliated him. To have a rough customer like Daniels feel privileged to pass any judgment on his wife—even admiration—galled him. To have old Ginn tell the directors in his holier-than-thou way what Clare should be required to do was utterly humiliating. Angus had managed a poker face, but his nerves had been exposed and raw as he listened to the talk. He had been forced to admit that he was resisted and defied in his own family. They all knew it now. And because he couldn't control his wife's activities, the company was losing money. A loss of nearly nine per cent—the worst showing the corporation had faced percentage-wise since the depression.

Tonight they'd have it out again. Instead of going back to peace, to dignity, to love, he was going home to renew the battle that had been going on for weeks. He would have to try again, put it up to her, tell her that the corporation was suffering a nine-per-cent drop in sales and that he felt completely responsible because his wife was the cause of it. Herb had said so flatly. Charley Sanders had admitted it, with considerable embarrassment. In cities all over the country salesmen were talking it over in bars, complaining that they were up against the ax because Mrs. Angus Baird was advising women not to have children. Ignorant Irish priests were denouncing her—and even if they didn't dare do it by name, everyone knew who was meant.

What devil had got into her? She'd never been like this about anything before. If they had disagreed she had always been the one to say, "Let's not argue about it—it's not that important. If you feel that way I won't wear it" . . . "won't do it" . . . "won't ask him to dinner" or whatever else it was that had caused some little clash of wills or opinions. But now she couldn't see reason—she didn't make sense. It had been a ghastly fortnight of new approaches, of his angers, of her silences, or that repeated "I'm sorry but I can't." Tonight she must give in. He had these figures, which surely would convince her of the seriousness of the situation and her obvious duty to resign from that job. She would—but what if she wouldn't?

Then she should be made to see a doctor. Or a psychiatrist. That idea had nibbled at Baird more than once lately, and it was one more shock and humiliation. Plenty of their friends needed analysis or had mental breakdowns. But he and Clare were balanced people. He'd always taken that for granted.

During his forty-three years Angus Baird had been able to take many things for granted, among them a background of money, exceptional health and secure position. He had been well educated and proved himself able to absorb education. He had learned and practiced almost every sport that men enjoyed. He could sit a horse, swing a golf club or cast a fly with equal skill and pleasure.

None of that had made him pompous. He had been forced to shoulder heavy responsibilities when his father died, for he was the only son. Before that, he had faced death himself in the war. Angus Baird had never thought that the world was his oyster. He had not been brought up to dodge work or run away from trouble. But the temperament which had been sunny when he was a boy had not basically changed as he grew older. He liked living, every day of it. He wanted to do the best job he could with his own life.

His grandfather and father had built a solid fortune. They had gone from farmlands to food products, building great canneries. The tradition of the Bairds was aristocratic and responsible, in a squirelike way. They knew what was expected of people who had money, and they met the expectations, living well themselves and giving generously. But they did not concern themselves with the machinery of good works. When the Baird men were not working at their own business, they preferred hunting in Canada or fishing off the Florida coast to attending committee meetings. And their wives always had several big establishments to keep handsome and hospitable.

When Angus met Clare Melander he wanted to marry her almost at once. He was then in the first of his thirties and as eligible as a man could be. The fact that he had not married earlier had not been due to either shyness with women or oversophistication. He had played around and raised the hopes of a good many girls. But he was serious about marriage. He wanted his marriage to be for keeps. Until he met Clare he had not seen any girl who made him sure that he would always want to keep her.

Clare's family was less wealthy than the Bairds, but it was even more distinguished. Her grandfather had been governor of his state and then ambassador to Switzerland. Her father was the head of a greatly respected law firm, a witty, fearless, erudite man. Both he and his wife were socially brilliant, and never provincial. They sent Clare, who was their only child and greatly prized and loved, to school in Virginia, and when she was through with that she made her debut at a Christmas party which was remembered for years for its exceptional gaiety and high style. Angus Baird was there, of course, and soon set his mind on marrying her. He had to wait. Clare tried a year of college, which was long enough to prove that she was very intelligent but an indifferent student. She spent the following year in France to please her father and mother and then came home and married Angus Baird. That was to please herself. She loved him as completely and confidently as he did her. "Those two were made for each other and there never was a more handsome couple" was the remark that many guests made at the wedding.

Angus had wished many times in the last two weeks that Clare's parents were still alive. He would have had them to consult with, their influence to add to his own. But they had been lost together when a luxury plane went down in the Atlantic some years before. Clare had been pregnant with her second child at the time, and Angus had been very apprehensive when he had to break the dreadful news to her.

Sometimes during this last fortnight he had been uncomfortably reminded of the way she had looked during the weeks after the tragedy. Her silence, her stillness, her almost abnormal control had not been peace but concealed struggle. After she heard the facts and knew with finality that there was no hope, Clare had talked very little even to Angus about her parents' death.

Once she said, "I wish I knew what my father said the very last thing. He would have summed it up." And several times, "They were together. They were glad of that."

There was no one in his own family to whom Angus could turn for backing now. He had three older sisters, but they were all married and lived in other cities. None of them had ever been close to Clare. He could not ask his mother—who had made the South Carolina estate her home since she was widowed—to interfere in this matter. And Herbert Martin had done all he could, to no avail.

He ran the car into one of the stalls in the garage and went through a side door into the lower floor of his house. The library was on this level, and in it several lamps were lit, though there was still enough twilight outside the long windows to show the color of the zinnias and chrysanthemums in the cutting garden, where Clare seemed to be able to make anything bloom. This was their favorite room, with its walls of books, one low shelf of them chosen for the children. The backgammon table was ready for a game, the fire of white birch logs laid on ancient andirons with Hessian figures, and the chair covered with scarlet satin was where Clare usually sat, with her slim legs tucked under her. Angus stood looking at her place, loving the room unhappily. Did strangers matter more to Clare than her home, than himself? Why, for something that was none of her business, was she destroying the dignity and happiness of this?

Chapter 6

꧁꧂

The street on which Mrs. Pearl Lemoy lived seemed completely unplanned. It glanced off from one of the main arteries in the city's industrial section, ran downhill in a wavering pattern for a dozen blocks, swerved around a corner and stopped, because it had to, on the edge of a stony, vacant area. Beyond that the waters of the harbor tossed, looking today as polluted as they undoubtedly were. It was stormy autumn weather and the roughened waves came in mud-colored, and with debris riding on them that even the gulls ignored.

As it went along, Morris Street had dropped a gas station on the first corner past the artery, a shop with an askew sign labeled ANTIQUES in its window to explain some broken chairs and glass kerosene lamps, a building which must have attempted to be a small factory half a century before and was now a broken-windowed wreck, and a number of small, perilous-looking houses. They were not identical, but most of them had peaked little gables, and they all were merged by neglect into a neighborhood that looked as if all pride of ownership was gone. But people were living in them. There were curtains and strips of shade cloth behind the rusty screens in the windows, bicycles propped against fences, television antennas stuck in the roofs, and here and there a car was parked, its white or green or yellow paint still gleaming.

Anne Milner had never been on this street before. She had not even known it was there until she studied a map of the city. She drove slowly, trying to avoid the worst potholes in the exhausted pavement, looking for number 1215 and gathering together in her mind all she knew about Mrs. Lemoy from studying the data in Carl Porada's office.

She had two legitimate children, and the oldest was a girl of sixteen. But long ago Pearl Lemoy's husband had deserted her. It must have been at least twelve years ago, for she had been on the county relief rolls for that long. Her oldest illegitimate child was eleven and she had brought three more into the world out of wedlock. The record had said briefly, "Presumably different fathers."

The oldest girl had become pregnant while she was a sophomore in high school and married the boy who admitted that he was responsible. But later he had run away—"Address of Joe Hart unknown," stated the cold case history—and Jenny Lemoy Hart, as a deserted widow, was now also getting aid for her dependent child.

Anne's nerves were tingling almost to the point of dread as she looked for the house number. This assignment was far more difficult and bewildering than she could have dreamed it would be. She had no experience in dealing with the kind of people she had been seeking out in the last two days and no protective shell of social-work training. She had spent a very difficult hour with a half-fawning, half-irate Mrs. Johnson, who told her that in California the relief payments were much larger and that the surplus foods which were doled out to her in this county were not fit for a dog. "You want to smell them eggs?" asked Mrs. Johnson. She also said that her oldest illegitimate child was going blind and she ought to get more money for him because the boy was sure going to lose his eyes. Mrs. Johnson had a very superior television set in her room.

It had been sickening to Anne to visit the Morans' cottage because Mrs. Moran was obviously incompetent to care for her four forlorn bastards, all less than seven years old. She was weak-minded enough to keep bearing them, but the record had stated that she was not an institutional case. As Anne left that place, a neighbor, who must have been watching, had run out to find out who the visitor was and to say that Mrs. Moran was a whore.

To get information out of the Jarvey family, who were on her list, was difficult. To trust the truth of what she did get was even harder. Mrs. Jarvey said the county welfare people were always snooping. If she tried to earn a little money, "helping out some lady," the county would dock her relief, said Mrs. Jarvey bitterly. She didn't go out to work any more. She didn't earn anything. All she had was from the welfare. But that didn't ring true. The Jarvey family seemed to be living fairly well. When one of the children said something about "Where's Pa?" her mother jerked her and said, "She's always imagining, this kid. She don't even remember her pa, he's been gone for seven years."

Anne had material enough. This would be the last of her interviews. But she thought with dismay of having to write the story. What would her angle be? What did she want to say?

There was the house. The second numeral had been lost from the number by the door, but that must be the right place. Anne parked her car and went up on the slanting porch. Someone had written BELL DOES NOT RING over the blackened, old-fashioned push button. She thought, it couldn't be expected to ring, and knocked.

She could hear a rushing sound of children inside and then several of them seemed to open the door simultaneously. Three of them stared at her with excitement and a baby crawled along the floor after them. And then a woman appeared through the doorway at the end of the room. She was obviously pregnant and Anne guessed that she might be thirty-five or -six years old.

Anne asked, "Are you Mrs. Lemoy?"

"That's right, dear," said the other.

72

"Could I come in and talk to you for a few minutes?"

"I don't know why not," said Pearl Lemoy, "if you can break through them children. Come here, kids. Jack, Chris! Don't swarm on the lady!" She stooped and picked up the baby and said, "I'll put this one inside his fence, where he'll be out of trouble. If it's selling something, I'm sorry, but I'm not able to buy much right now. But sit down, anyway. It's nice to have someone come in on a dark, mean day like this."

Anne sat down. She did not glance around the room at once. But she felt a kind of easygoing comfort in it. She sorted out the children by name while Mrs. Lemoy settled the infant in a playpen patched with cardboard on one side. And she realized as she watched the woman move about and come back to seat herself on the edge of a ragged sofa that Pearl Lemoy was a beautiful woman. Incredibly, still beautiful and no doubt a woman tempting to men. Her jumper was blue, almost the exact sea blue of her rather languid eyes, her skin was flawless and her hair made Anne think of Joyce. Or was it because Joyce also carried herself with pride when she was pregnant?

"No, I'm not selling anything," she said, "I just want to ask a big favor of you, Mrs. Lemoy. I'd like to ask a few questions. Would you tell me how you feel about the work the county is doing for people like yourself who need a little help now and then?"

The friendly hospitality of Pearl Lemoy went into retreat. Her face changed and became masked with wariness. She almost cringed as she said, "Oh, you're from the welfare."

"No, I'm not. Actually I work on the morning newspaper. And I'm going around visiting people to get some reactions—opinions from clients of the welfare—to find out whether you think what's being done is necessary and done in the right way."

"The welfare people are awful sore at me," said Pearl Lemoy, still in that daunted tone.

"Why should they be?"

"Oh, you can't hardly blame them. In one way. All the kids. They think it's awful. But I don't know. I can see how they feel, but just the same . . ." She stopped, as if expression came too hard, and smiled again at Anne, with a kind of charming, guilty helplessness.

"Will you tell me something about yourself? I don't want to seem nosy," said Anne, "but . . ."

"That's all right. They've got it all put down on paper up there at the courthouse. They'd tell you. Why, about me, I had some bad luck but some good luck too. Every one of my kids is healthy—most of them smart, too. I hate to have them sore at me at the welfare, but you know, dear, the way I see it things will work out—that's what I always say—things work out if you give them time."

It was certainly difficult not to like Pearl Lemoy. But she's slept with all those men, thought Anne—the different fathers. She must be a little half-witted, if not worse.

"I was married, you know," explained Pearl. "We did fine for a while, too. With the first two kids. Then we moved here and he lost his job that he came here for and then he got to drinking and I don't know—sometimes you blame a man and sometimes you think they don't have it so easy either. And they know that if they skip out, the welfare may give you better than they can—I know that was what was in his mind when he skipped."

It was what Anne had been told to investigate. There it was, in so many words from a woman who surely ought to know.

"And he never came back?"

"Oh, Lord no, dear, he's probably at the other end of the country by now. He liked to travel—always talking about Texas or Mexico. He didn't like the climate here, that was one thing. He wouldn't never come back. He wouldn't have the fare."

"Did you divorce him?"

74

"I guess I could have. Some say you can, some say you can't. You see, I'm a Catholic."

"So am I," said Anne.

"That's nice, dear," said Pearl Lemoy approvingly.

"And you really can get a legal divorce if you're a Catholic. The only thing is that you can't marry again."

"That's what the priest told me. He talked to me. He said I could get a divorce. But it's expensive, dear. And if you can't marry any more, what's the good of it?"

Anne said hesitantly, "It's none of my business, but do you feel right about having all these other children without being married?"

Pearl Lemoy laughed. Not coarsely. It was the laugh of realism. She said, "Well, dear, you know men. But as they say, we wouldn't want to get along without them. Men always took after me since I was no bigger than that. And one thing, I never had a man treat me cruel. Of course, they aren't free themselves as a usual thing—some woman's hanging on to them for dear life even if she knows they'd rather have you."

"I can certainly understand why they take after you. But to have children when you know they won't have a father to look after them—it's a pretty big risk, isn't it? You think it's fair to them?"

"What are you going to do?" Pearl tossed the question back. "You know, I've thought about that. Every time I get caught. And sometimes I thought I'd go to that clinic place uptown and get stuff or have them do something to me. I guess they'll even do it free. But they say it changes a woman, that it ages her. And of course it's against the Church. They're always talking about that, that it's a sin to do anything to stop it. I go to church. When I can. Jenny is very religious too. You know, this baby in the pen is Jenny's boy. Jenny's gone somewhere today looking for work and she left him with me."

"So that's your daughter Jenny's child? Your grandson?"

Pearl giggled. "Sounds funny—me with a grandson. Yes, that's him. Believe me, I was awful mad when that happened to her. Jenny was smart as a whip. She wanted to be a teacher and she could have. I said to her, 'Jenny, we may be good Catholics, but just the same I think you ought to do something to get rid of it.' But she said, 'No, Mom, I want it. And getting rid of it is the worst sin of all.' He was a Catholic boy too, you know. And they were married, so it wasn't so bad. The priest got after Joe and said he had to marry Jenny. You'd like Jenny. I wish she was here to meet you. When they broke up she said, 'Joe'll do better without me and I'll do better on the welfare.' We get along. She gets hers for the baby, and I'll get $23.10 more when this one comes out of the oven. I always feel good when I'm carrying a baby—some women don't, but I do."

"That's certainly lucky."

"What's the use of fussing?" asked Pearl Lemoy philosophically. "That's the way the Lord made women—so they could. I like kids. And they grow up before you know it. Here's Jenny a married woman and Rex—they're true brother and sister, those two—he says he's going to go through High. He's learning typewriting. Luke's smart, too—he's the other one. But poor Luke, the truant officer's awful down on him."

"How old is Luke?"

Pearl figured. "He's eleven."

That one. The oldest illegitimate child. You are a wonderful, blithe animal, thought Anne, listening to Pearl Lemoy. You are a menace to the public and to your children and you're delightful. She said, "I must be on my way. But I can't tell you how glad I am to have met you and had a little talk."

"Me too," said Pearl, "I just love company. And I haven't got anything against the welfare. Sometimes it seems they could give people a little more—things are awful high. If I didn't get a little present now and then, I don't know how the kids and I could get along. But I don't bear the welfare no grudge, though some say they put too much in their own pockets. Would you like a cup of coffee? I was just going to make some when you come in."

"Thanks, but I must get back to work." Anne made her way through the children, who swarmed again until she closed the door. She drove into the stone field to turn around because the street was so narrow, and as she passed the Lemoy house again she saw a boy coming toward it, a handsome boy with a slow, hippy, light-footed walk, head high, eyes rather insolent as they looked her over. Probably Luke, she thought, on his way home from trouble.

When she reached the center of the city, Anne stopped at a drugstore, not so much for the coffee she ordered as for a pause to think over what she had just seen and heard. She found herself wishing that she could talk with Carl Porada. He had seemed inconsistent, but now she understood that. There was no possible doubt that there were some women on relief who exploited desertion and illegitimacy at county expense. It was his job to expose that. But Carl Porada had said to her rather angrily, "I don't want to parade the poor creatures through the streets in your newspaper or anywhere else."

Neither do I, thought Anne. I'm mixed up, too. This is a wonderful human-interest story—it's just what Max Fleming wanted—but I don't know the answer. I wasn't told to find the answer—Max said the paper wouldn't take a stand. It's Carl Porada's job to come up with some solution. I wonder how that man happened to go into politics. He isn't the smooth type. I wonder if he ever saw Pearl Lemoy.

She thought of Pearl Lemoy saying that no man had ever treated her cruel. Pearl slept with men and liked it. She enjoyed intercourse and always felt good when there was a baby in her womb. That was what women were for. Anne thought, I don't believe there is a mean bone in Pearl Lemoy's body. She made me feel like a tight-laced, inexperienced old maid. It's horrible to think of what goes on in that shack—what those children must see—but there's pleasure. . . .

She's only thirty-five. She'll probably have at least four or five more children. She should be sterilized. Carl Porada said that couldn't be put over, that the birth control people ought to get busy here. I must try to find out how much work their clinic here does with women who are on relief. If I can find out anything, I'll tell him. I'll probably never see him again, but I could write him a note. I ought to thank him again for the liberal education I'm getting—due to him.

She slid off her stool and paid her check. The birth control clinic was not far away. Anne had never been inside it, but she knew that it was housed in a neat little building close to the municipal hospital. She decided to go there immediately and ask a few questions of whoever was in charge of the place. Clare Baird came into Anne's mind. If what Max Fleming had said about her association with birth control doing harm to her husband's business was true, she would certainly give up that work. Perhaps she had done so already.

A waiting room opening off a long hallway was piped with music and furnished cheerfully. Several women were apparently waiting their turn for consultation or treatment. The face of one was familiar to Anne, and she was careful not to look at her twice. She went to the desk where a young receptionist sat. This girl couldn't have a better manner for her job, thought Anne. Friendly, frank and serene—a manner which said reassuringly that planned parenthood is nothing to be ashamed of.

"Would you like to register?" asked the girl pleasantly.

"No, thank you. I'm not a patient. My name is Anne Milner and I'm women's editor for the *Observer*. If it's possible, I wanted to get a little information for a story that we are going to run."

"About our work? Yes, indeed. We have a number of pamphlets I'd be glad to give you. This one on the population explosion is probably the most comprehensive. It tells what we are trying to do all over the world."

"I'd like very much to read it. But what I'm interested in

for this particular story," said Anne, "are facts about your local clients. I wonder if you could tell me how many are on the relief rolls."

"I'm sorry. All our records are completely confidential."

"I wouldn't use any names," persisted Anne, "and I think the story would call the attention of a great many people to what you are doing here. One of our important public officials said to me the other day that he hoped you were working with women on relief." She paraphrased what Carl Porada had said persuasively.

The serene girl looked thoughtful. She said, "I couldn't give out that information myself. But perhaps you could talk to Mrs. Baird, the chairman of our Governing Board."

"Is she here?"

"I think she's in her office."

"Would she see me for a few minutes?"

"I'll find out." The receptionist pressed the button of the intercom and said, "Mrs. Baird, Anne Milner is here from the *Observer*. She wants some information. Could you see her?"

There was only the briefest pause. Then, "Thank you, Mrs. Baird. I'll send her right in. It is the last door at the end of the hall, Miss Milner."

The last door opened on a tiny office. The single desk held baskets of letters, a dictaphone and a bowl of multicolored anemones. Clare Baird wore a white silk blouse open at the throat, and a yellow sweater was tossed loosely over her shoulders. To Anne she seemed much thinner than she had looked on the platform at the convention and there were shadows under her eyes. But her indestructible distinction was as Anne had seen and felt it before.

"You're very good to see me."

"Oh, I wanted to see you," Clare Baird said, and Anne felt that she was being seen very completely, measured mentally, decided upon.

"Is this the first time you've visited the clinic?"

"Yes. I was on vacation when it opened. But I heard you speak at the convention recently. It was a very interesting talk."

"I saw your story about the meeting."

"I hope you thought I covered it all right."

"Yes, it was very accurate," said Clare Baird, remembering that morning, that terrible breakfast when the struggle had begun. But it wasn't the fault of this surprisingly attractive girl.

She asked, "What kind of information do you want from us—is it Miss or Mrs. Milner?"

"It's just Anne. I'm not married, but no one on a newspaper or radio or television ever has a last name."

"So mass communications destroy it?"

"That's right." They laughed and liked each other more.

"I'm interested in what actually goes on here," Anne said. "I feel very fortunate in having a chance to talk to you personally. There are conflicting rumors, you know."

"I know."

"And I'd especially like to find out what kind of women your patients are—clients—I don't know what to call them."

"The name doesn't matter. And there are many different kinds of women. The thing they have in common is that they are all looking for information or supplies—often both—which they find it hard or impossible to get anywhere else. Here they get professional advice from the nurses on our staff or are referred to doctors. The people who work in the clinic are almost all professionals—except for a few people like myself."

"But you're the chairman."

"As far as organization goes—yes."

"The way a civilian heads up the War Department?"

Clare Baird laughed. "I have some small usefulness. But it's our staff that fights the war. They examine the women who come to the clinic, not of course unless they ask for that, and then each woman is advised about methods and what may be most practical for her—the pill, the foam, the ring . . . or rhythm."

"That too?"

"Of course. Though we don't guarantee that method. What we don't do—you say you have heard rumors—we do not sterilize women. We don't treat women who are already pregnant. We don't perform abortions. We try to make the ones who want help more serene and secure in their sex relations and able to plan their families. We believe in families," Clare Baird said, "that's why we're here."

"You give out contraceptives?"

"Of course."

"Do you charge for them?"

"If a woman can pay."

"And if they can't?"

"We take care of them."

"That's one of the things I wanted to find out. I've been on an assignment which raises a lot of questions." Anne explained it, told what she had seen and heard, and Clare Baird listened with such interest that the story took on color and even humor.

Anne came to the point. "So it obviously is true that there are at least some women who accept desertion, or even connive at it with their husbands, because they think they can live on relief better than independently. Some of them are willing to have illegitimate children—or they're easily reconciled to it— because there is an allowance for each dependent child. But I didn't think that many of the women I saw were evil—there was sharp practice all right, and some of them were certainly below-par mentally. . . ."

"So they shouldn't have children. . . ."

"But they will," said Anne. "The ones like that never get here. What I've been wondering is how large a percentage of women on relief do come to your clinic. I don't want to write anything that exaggerates the situation."

"Many of them come. You'll be telling the truth if you say that many dependent parents want to have small families and only need to know how to manage it."

Anne asked, not because she would write about it but because she wanted to know, "Are some of those parents Catholics?"

"We don't ask whether they are Catholics or not. If we did, I wouldn't trust the answers. Women who are Catholics might not admit it. You can understand why. You can't blame them. Their Church is so strongly opposed to this work."

"I know. I'm a Catholic."

"Are you really? I'm surprised."

"Why?"

Clare Baird hesitated, then said with disarming frankness, "From that story you wrote about the convention I somehow got the impression that you were rather sympathetic with what we're doing. Not that the report said so, but I thought I read it between the lines. I must have been quite wrong."

"I did think that you had more facts than the ones who voted against the resolution and were less emotional. In a way I was sympathetic. To tell the truth"—Anne was yielding to impulse—"I'm mixed up about what I do think of birth control. Especially after some of the things I saw and heard while I was working on this story. But I can't go along with it unless I defy my own Church. I couldn't give up my religion. It's easy for people like yourself to support birth control, because there's no conflict for you—you don't have to give up anything for it."

A strange expression crossed Clare Baird's face. Was it derision? Misery? Anne was not sure what it was, and in less than a second the look was gone. But what had caused it was obvious. It was a vivid rejection of Anne's assumption that the other woman did not have to sacrifice anything for this project in which she was involved. In Anne's mind other things

82

fell into place and made a pattern now. She had been right in her first impression this afternoon. Clare Baird was thinner. She had lost the confident buoyancy, the obvious joy of crusading that had been evident when she spoke to the club-women. What Max Fleming had said was probably true. Clare Baird's connection with the birth control movement was hurting her husband's business and she knew it.

Clare said, "Thank you for saying that you might be with us if you could. It really is encouraging. You know, we constantly hope that your Church will change its point of view."

"That's not likely."

"But it seemed to me—until recently—that many Catholics had begun to see the need for family planning. Obviously you yourself do."

"Even if you see the problems, that doesn't change what we are taught, told over and over again—that artificial birth control breaks a law of nature. And because it is a natural law, it can never be changed."

"Surely any law can be changed. It should be when it's creating misery."

Anne said in a baffled way, "It's so hard to understand unless you are a Catholic. With us natural law isn't made by human beings. It's made by God and is put into people when they are created. So even the highest churchmen can't change a natural law because it's not possible to undo what God has done. That's oversimplification, but it's the basic doctrine. For example, the Pope and the College of Cardinals could make it all right for Catholics to eat meat on Friday if they wanted to do that, because fasts like that are decreed by men at the head of the Church. But no one in the hierarchy can alter the natural law."

"It's so strange—rather obscure to me."

"What it gets down to," said Anne, trying again, "is that we believe that we have desires and appetites for certain purposes. And sex acts are for procreation."

83

"Only that?"

"There's no law against pleasure. Only against deliberately thwarting the purpose."

"Then how can Catholics allow rhythm? That thwarts it."

"No, that's restraint. You don't have to indulge an appetite."

"It seems like dancing on a needle. Begging the question."

"I suppose it does to you," said Anne helplessly, "but there it is."

"To me it's an unreasonable attitude in a Church which has more poor people in it than any other Christian one. That's what I've always admired about Catholicism—that it draws the poor all over the world into it and gives them comfort and something to hope for. Before I was married I spent a year in Europe and I loved to go into Catholic churches—not just the cathedrals but parish churches in the French and Austrian villages. I always felt welcome in them, though I didn't understand the symbols or the devotions. There was something generous and gentle—and profound, too—in the air in those places. I can see why frightened people have always sought sanctuary in Catholic churches. But what puzzles me is why a religion that's so identified with protection and shelter should try to block the way for the people who believe in it to have better lives."

"That's not what it means to do. Not what it wants."

"My father never went to any church," Clare said, "but I can remember his saying, 'If you can't be a Roman Catholic, why take anything less?' I'm telling you this to explain that I've always respected your Church—more than that. Until—well, I've been shocked lately by the bitterness of Catholics toward people who don't believe what they do. By their actions. I don't want to be rude . . ."

"You're not rude. I think I know what you mean and I'm terribly sorry. Rather ashamed. All of us aren't like that. But there isn't much use in talking about it."

84

"I thought there was use! I believed that if the Catholics would look at the facts squarely and discuss them with the rest of us, we'd find some answers. Something would come out of frank talk, even if it was only honest disagreement. But blows in the dark—blackmailing people who aren't involved, unbelievable, unsigned letters . . ." She looked at Anne questioningly. "I've heard that the priests denounce me from the pulpits—do they?"

"Some priests aren't very intelligent."

"Don't they have to be?"

"They can administer the Sacraments without being men you like or admire," said Anne. "If they happen to be bad-tempered or intolerant, they still can baptize us, marry us, bury us. . . ."

"And forbid you to prevent pregnancy."

"In artificial ways."

"No matter what—poverty, illness, bad mental history—none of those things makes any difference?"

"They don't make any difference," repeated Anne and heard her own small sigh. Was it audible to Clare Baird? It had been involuntary.

"Do you really think that's right?" Clare Baird did not ask that in a tone of argument but almost pleadingly, as if she needed help and sympathy.

Anne had to answer. She knew that she had been dodging the answer to that question even to herself. In this moment she was conscious of the barrier between herself and Clare Baird, between herself and every non-Catholic. No one except a Catholic understood the bondage and the support, the discipline and the ecstasy of feeling the will utterly free. She had come up against this barrier many times. Often in the university, when it was impossible to explain the compulsion to get up on every Sunday morning and possibly go through rain or a driving snow to attend Mass—and a hurried, dreary service it might be.

"Why can't you say your prayers right here?" some girl would ask.

"What will happen if you don't go?"

Nothing serious would happen. Only there would be a dullness of failure in her mind, dissatisfaction, distrust of herself. And when she confessed the lapse in attendance, some priest would admonish her with a brief sentence and tell her to say a penitential prayer that would take five minutes.

Her friends were sometimes curious about the confessional.

"But I'd rather die than tell a strange man intimate things about myself. Do you really do that? You know the kind of things I mean."

You did. Because to conceal or cheat was worse than telling it.

And they thought some things were comical, or absurd.

"There's nothing else fit to eat tonight. You'll starve if you don't take a piece of beef. Now, honestly, Anne, do you think that if there is a God, that He's watching somewhere to see whether you eat meat or not? I don't want to be rude, but isn't that rather primitive? That sort of thing is natural in emerging cultures but not among educated people. Look, it isn't Friday in Italy, it's Saturday—you could eat meat there. Why stuff yourself with carbohydrates here?"

You never can make it clear, Anne said to herself. But I have to answer Clare Baird.

She said, "To Catholics people aren't just human beings. They are individual souls even before they are born—even when they are witless or starving—and it is more important to save their souls than to prevent them from suffering as human beings. It's built into us that our souls are more important than our bodies or happiness or even decent living. I've had that preached to me since I was six years old. I think that one reason the Church is so opposed to birth control is because it makes material things more important than souls."

She paused, but Clare Baird was silent, as if she were not satisfied, and Anne went on.

"From the time we are very young—actually before we understand what a lot of the words mean—we hear in church that married people must not keep themselves from having children. As you get older you come out of the fog—or some boy tells you—and you know it's contraception that's being denounced. Some of the sermons are pretty wild and savage. I think they go too far and they get on the nerves of a great many Catholics. But that doesn't make any difference to some priests who believe that the most important thing they can do is to repeat the laws about childbearing."

"Their laws," Clare said, "not laws for people who don't think having children is an end in itself. I love children and I think the best job a woman can do is to have them if she's fit for it and in a position to bring them up well. Most of the people who come to this clinic have come to the same conclusion. And some of them were probably brought up in your Church."

"I know that's true. There's a woman in your waiting room this afternoon whom I've often seen in the cathedral. But even though she is here . . ." Anne let the fact stand and stopped talking. There was the barrier. How could she explain that the suffering or defiant woman wasn't a solution?

Clare Baird was thinking of something else. She said evenly, "I didn't ask her to come here. She came of her own free will. Why should I be persecuted for that?"

"You shouldn't be."

"The Catholics are trying to make it impossible for me to go on with this work. They are putting pressure on me through my husband's business. Did you know that?"

"I've heard some gossip. I think it's outrageous and I don't mind saying so."

A smile flashed toward her. "Thank you. That does help, coming from you. I'm going to tell you something—it's not for publication please. . . ."

"Of course not."

"Because I'm not going to answer them back. I'm not going

to get into any open fight, which is what they may want. But I'm not going to give up this job."

"You shouldn't. They have no right to do what they're doing."

Clare Baird said without raising her voice, with no touch of the dramatic, "It's not that I think I'm important or indispensable. When it was first suggested that I resign, I felt that if I did I would be running away, breaking promises, letting an organization down. So I said that I couldn't. But I didn't realize then what the consequences would be."

Almost as if to herself, she said, "I had no idea how this could hurt . . . other people. . . ."

She means her husband, thought Anne. This is tearing her to pieces.

"Maybe," Clare Baird said, "at one point I might have given in. But I began to see that I—or anything personal connected with me—wasn't the most important thing. This is a deliberate attempt to destroy the work—the idea of planning and caring for families. All over the world. You have your own kind of mysticism. I think this is mine. It's the thing that's beyond my own happiness. I have to sustain it. If I knuckle down, if they can beat me down—using my loyalties as weapons, and that's what they're doing—then they'll use the same methods to get rid of the next person—and the next one. A great many useful people might become afraid to do this work. And so if you hear any rumors of my resigning from this job, Anne, don't believe them."

Chapter 7

❧❧❧

Bishop Bolles was not a man to explore a situation quickly. Often he would wait until it exposed itself. He preferred to let his own decisions ripen and rarely interfered in matters over which his subordinates were supposed to have authority. But he was familiar with the personalities and abilities of every priest in his diocese, and tried out the young, new ones with the same patience that he displayed in dealing with the well-known faults and crotchets of some of the older members of his clergy.

Tonight Father Collins and Father Walker were dining with him. The Bishop had an excellent cook and it was always a treat to be asked to "the Palace," as the hierarchy humorously designated the huge, rambling red-brick house which a former Bishop had acquired through the generosity of a wealthy deceased widow. It was not a conference, but an occasion like this was never purely social. Both priests knew that before the evening was over some subject would be brought up which the Bishop wanted to recommend to their individual attention.

Over the meal they had talked only about the need for remodeling the Sisters' home, the annoyance of the streams of requests for Catholic projects which were not the obligations of this diocese but drained away money that it needed, and the possibility of getting a Catholic on the city library board who might check the purchase of obscene books with public money.

So the subject of literature was before them as they were drinking coffee—large cups of it with the cigars and cigarettes. The Bishop asked, "Father Collins, have you chanced to see the series of articles in *Future* on the Church and its attitude—perhaps I should say attitudes—toward birth control?"

"I read all six of them, Bishop," said Father Collins, "and I found them appalling. I have been hoping for an opportunity to ask you what plans have been made to refute them. They are surely the most insidious kind of propaganda, with their misquotations of Catholic doctrine and their playing up of the amateur theology of renegades. And they prove beyond any doubt that a malignant attack—with millions of dollars behind it—is under way again!"

"The articles weren't presented as an attack," said Father Walker. "They stated that with some emphasis. It's the population increase that seems to have been the motive that—"

"A pretense!" interrupted Father Collins. "A mask which we should drag off their faces and their arguments! These people aren't worried about the population of the world. What they're worried about is the increase in the number of Catholic converts—it's the old APA come to life again, and in sheep's clothing as usual."

"But a number of our clergy go along with them. They let themselves be quoted. And lay people of considerable standing—"

"The laity is always looking for an excuse to have it easy," said Father Collins.

He was a fiercely raw-boned man and once had been red-haired, for though his head was now covered with a resistant gray thatch, there was a sunset color in it. He was flushed with indignation, and his hands struck small unrhythmic blows on the arms of his chair as he spoke. The young priest sitting opposite him had a narrow, thoughtful face. He seemed less sure of words than Father Collins, but the Bishop, gnawing his cigar and watching them both, wondered if Father Walker were not firmly disagreeing with everything Father Collins said.

The Bishop himself was a large man, though not fat. The loosened skin on his cheeks and neck showed the ravages caused by middle-aged dieting. His bearing, even in repose, held the dignity of one used to receiving homage and his superb diction proved scholarship. But sometimes a little coaxing brogue crept into his accents, suggesting simplicity and humor when simplicity was desirable or humor necessary. The brogue was quite audible now.

"The Church will never be harmed by any argument," he said, "whether it be at this little supper table or in the pages of a magazine. But I often think that our late, beloved Pope left us with a very difficult task when he bade us cope with the social and economic changes that are pervading the world."

The young priest's eyes lit up and he was on the verge of saying something, but Father Collins was quicker.

"Changes there may be, but never in the natural law," he stated.

Father Walker leaned forward. "The natural law is being reexamined even in our seminaries. Some very sound theologians have said that St. Thomas himself held that nature and reason can be at times in conflict. Primitive nature differs from modern nature. I recently read this statement: 'Out of the living Church and supernatural life come new applications of the truths of faith which in each generation are assimilated into that long tradition which is the history of the Church.' I memorized the exact words, for they seemed so wise that I wanted to use them in a sermon."

"Memorizing the words of heretics, Father?" inquired Father Collins.

The young priest grinned. "No, those are the words of Cardinal Cushing."

Bishop Bolles did not smile at the expense of Father Collins. He spoke gravely and very directly to him.

"We need men like you, Father," he said. "In a world that is so fluid we need priests with conviction. We need the ones who will dig in their heels. The ones who will say, 'Prove it to me and then prove it to me again before I will depart from a tenet long held true. And probably I shall find myself unable to depart from it, no matter what you argue.' In ancient Rome they made martyrs of men like you, Father."

Father Collins looked flustered and pleased. Father Walker gazed at the tablecloth and listened with a stubborn expression.

"But in modern Rome," the Bishop went on, "when I was there several months ago, I found a situation that would have been incredible in the days when I was a student in Vatican City. Conversations are going on in high places about these very matters of population increase and the prevention of conception. And the conversations—which are said to be courteous and mutually respectful—are in many cases between members of the Catholic clergy and frank advocates of artificial birth control."

"Aren't such conversations very sensible?" asked Father Walker.

"Possibly," said the Bishop dryly, "possibly not. I was more impressed—and troubled—by my own talks with some of our faith who have risen to eminence in foreign countries. These men are greatly disturbed by the increase of their native populations, and from what they told me they have good reason to be. Ours is such an immensely rich country that in spite of gloomy predictions I personally believe we can absorb a growing population. I believe that in North America Catholic emphasis should be placed on devising ways to care for all children—to feed them all, to educate them all according to their abilities and to instruct them in good habits of life. I think that can be done here, though it may take time and great courage."

"That is what I constantly preach to my congregation," said Father Collins.

"I'm glad to hear it. But we cannot close our eyes to the fact that in some other countries there are problems of space and finance which are more serious than any that confront us here. I was told that in many places there is evasion, indifference and resistance to the traditional teaching of the Church about the sin of artificial birth control."

He paused to relight his cigar, and Father Walker said, "That's true in South America. I found that there many Catholics ignore the prohibition. They think it's unreasonable and that the priests don't really mean what they say."

"Priests should make it clear that they do mean it," said Father Collins.

Bishop Bolles went on as if neither of the others had spoken. "We can only abide by the doctrines of the Church. We must so instruct our parishes."

"I would refuse to marry a couple who intimated to me that they considered limitation of their family."

"You stretch the law too far, Father," said the Bishop mildly. "Limitation is allowed for proper reasons and in licit ways."

"Yes, but give them an inch and they take an ell," said Father Collins grimly.

"But in the modern world," protested Father Walker, suddenly pricked into volubility, "with the cost of living what it is and housing often so difficult to find, an old-fashioned family, with ten or twelve children, can't make ends meet. Today people—most of them—have to live in apartments, not on farms. We haven't room in our schools—"

"Specious arguments," said Father Collins, with contempt for them.

The Bishop took over again. He said, "Studies are being made. Our President has approved increased research in fertility. If God inspires such research, a way may be found to reconcile the natural law with the modern problems that seem to weigh so heavily on Father Walker. But that time has not come."

"I know that, Bishop. I did not mean—"

"No matter," said Bishop Bolles. He never pursued an argument with those bound to yield in respect to him. "We know our duty and we must not fail it. However, our responsibility is to those of our own faith and not to our non-Catholic brothers. Indeed"—the brogue was stronger—"if they limit their families sufficiently, there may be more room on earth for good Catholics."

He chuckled and Father Walker grinned boyishly, but the other priest wore a stony expression. He sensed where this was leading. He guessed that the Bishop had not been idly conversing on this subject but that he was laying a foundation for something pertinent to his own diocese and the men who had dined with him. And here it came.

"In any case, the present temper is one of patience as we await the results of research under government and other auspices. If we cannot in conscience co-operate or go along with it, we can demonstrate our patience and toleration of efforts that are well-meaning even if ill advised. Clerical circles at a high level set this example, as I have said."

He let that sink in, then became definite.

"Lately I have been wondering about my own bailiwick. Gossip—I hope that is all it amounts to—has come to me about the instigation of boycotts against business firms because their officers, or members of the families of these officers, promote birth control activity. Your ears are closer to the ground than mine are. Is there any truth in such rumors?"

"Yes, Bishop," said Father Walker, "there's a lot of feeling against the Baird Company. The baby-food manufacturers."

"What's wrong with their pap?" asked the Bishop. "I don't have it in my own larder, naturally."

94

Father Walker controlled his own smile and tucked that remark away for quotation in the proper quarters.

"It's not the stuff they make," he said, "it's Mrs. Baird, the wife of the president of the company, who's under fire. She's a very big shot in the planned-parenthood movement—that's what they call it. She makes speeches about it and runs this clinic in town where the women are told what to do."

"Where, no doubt, many women are sterilized," remarked Father Collins icily.

"It seems somewhat far-fetched to blame the Baird Company. It's a national concern."

"It hits them where they feel it. I hear that the sales of their food have fallen off not just here in the city but in many places all over the country." There was a note of triumph in Father Collins' remark.

"Then there must be some sort of organization?"

"Chain letters," Father Walker told the Bishop bluntly. "I know it was suggested to some of the sodalities that their members contact relatives and people they know elsewhere. The old method—one person writes a letter to ten people and each of them is asked to write to ten others. You can start quite a prairie fire that way, especially in a case like this, when nobody had to put in any money." He did not look at Father Collins as he explained it.

"Ah," said the Bishop thoughtfully, "I suspected something of that sort was going on."

And he had, since Mrs. Ginn had called on him recently. She had not asked him to write letters. She had said, "I know how widespread your influence is, Bishop Bolles, and if you would say a word here and there to your revered colleagues, it would be invaluable. Confidentially, Bishop, my husband has urged the board of directors of the Baird Company to insist that Clare Baird give up these things she is doing. She has refused. It is not the financial loss that troubles Lucius as much as the bad reputation she is giving the company."

The Bishop had said pleasantly as always, "This lady is not under my discipline. I fail to see what I can do about the problem."

"If the financial pressure is strong enough, she will have to behave herself," Mrs. Ginn had said.

Her words had been sharp, though she invariably looked like a saint. A very pious lady. A generous lady to the Church, though in ways which she herself chose and would show to her credit. The Bishop would have preferred a modern wing on the shabby home for the nuns to the chimes and the beautiful stained-glass windows. A vengeful lady she had seemed when she spoke of Mrs. Baird. Was there more to it, the Bishop wondered, than defense of her religion? Social jealousies had run deep in this city for many years.

"So the hostility is directed at Mrs. Angus Baird," said the Bishop musingly, as if he had just found that out. Both priests were aware that he had probably looked into this with his customary thoroughness. "I've not had the privilege of meeting the lady. I believe she was the Melander girl. The only child. That was sad—both parents killed in an accident over the sea. I knew her father. An extraordinary chess player. A heathen. We had a little game of chess now and then at the Old Town Club, and he said to me one day, 'Bishop, I can't accept your religion, but I promise not to go along with any of the splinters and shavings from it.' Well, that's neither here nor there, and I've kept you lingering when I know you have early duties tomorrow." He rose from the table and led them to the dining-room door.

"Good night, Father Walker. Good night, Father Collins." He extended his hand and they kissed the ring. "God bless you. You have your little vehicles?"

The two priests exchanged a further brief good night on the sidewalk and started their small cars in different directions. Father Walker had been assigned during the last year to a small, debt-ridden church in a district not far from the water-front. It was his first pastorate—from the seminary he had been sent to a mission in Ecuador—and its problems were always in the forefront of his thoughts. Problems of unemployment and overcrowding and delinquencies—he heard them in the confessional and saw them in the faces of his unreliable congregation.

He was often an angry young man underneath that hesitant manner. But tonight he was warm with satisfaction and with admiration of his Bishop. There had been no word of praise, and yet he felt encouraged. He felt conscious of backing and understanding. Driving through streets with dim, dreary lights swinging here and there on sagging posts, past little houses that were so obviously inadequate, he thought, the Bishop knows that the world has to be better than this. Living in the Palace doesn't fool him. He knows that there must be change and that the Church has to go along with it. He parked his car in front of his rectory, a cottage which was no better than any of the others in the same block. A drunken man was coming down the street, and Father Walker recognized him as belonging to his own parish. This man did not come often to Mass—he was probably sleeping it off every Sunday morning—but his wife came. She had seven children and worked by the day as long as she could between her pregnancies. The man stumbled on a crack in the pavement. Father Walker took his elbow and steadied him to the door of his house, down the street.

Father Collins now had a stall for his automobile, for the cathedral had a handsome modern rectory. It was the finest residence in which the priest had ever lived. He had been one of twelve children and had fought his way from poverty to the dignity and security of Holy Orders. He went through a covered passage and entered the beautiful hallway of the rectory. He never ceased to admire it, and he had a right to do so, for he had been the driving force in raising the money for building both the cathedral and the rectory ten years before. He admired the monastic length of the hallway now as he wondered if the Bishop planned to transfer him.

There had been no rebuke. But it was clear enough that Bishop Bolles did not approve of what the priest had been doing or saying. He had been warned to desist. But I am right, thought Father Collins. The Bishop may send me where he pleases, when he pleases. I shall never complain. I shall go on doing the work of God. I shall teach the Law. One day the Church will regret this toleration of evil.

The telephone on a marble table rang and he picked it up.

"Cathedral Rectory. Father Collins speaking."

"Father, this is Everett Moore. My wife—she's here at the hospital. I'm telephoning from the hospital—they're afraid she's going—" The voice broke.

Father Collins asked, "Is it the child?"

"Yes, the child's born. Will you come at once, Father? She doesn't want just the chaplain—she's asking for you, Father."

"At once," said Father Collins. His voice was tender and reassuring. "Tell Cecilia I'm coming and that I'll be praying for her every inch of the way. Tell her that the Blessed Mother is watching over her and praising her, Everett."

Chapter 8

~~~~~

It was November and the city by the great lake was facing the ordeal of its long winter. The snows had not yet come and that made the leafless trees and frostbitten lawns seem very stark. A few ships still braved the weather, and on a stormy night like this one the foghorns moaned incessantly. Rain during the day had turned to driving sleet as darkness came, and pedestrians and motorists got under cover as soon as they could, knowing how hazardous the streets would be. The occasional siren of an ambulance or fire engine screaming on their way to disasters seemed more ominous than usual. It was a night when people would be wakened by rattling windows and creaking doors and kept awake by worry. A night for restlessness, especially if a person was alone.

Carl Porada lived alone. He had not meant it to be that way when he bought the house on the North Shore Drive. He had thought that Alys would live there with him. The house had been just what he wanted, and he had been ingenuous enough to believe—in the beginning—that a girl he loved would like what he did.

The house was several miles beyond the city limits. It was a sturdy structure of shingle and fieldstone, as it had to be to survive its location on a hillock only five hundred feet from the beach, where agates and crystal thomsonites often gleamed among the pebbles and curious shapes of driftwood bleached. It had been built by an architect who must have valued space and variation highly, for the only neighbors were spruce trees and the lake was constantly changing its mood. He had meant to live there himself when he retired, and had finished and almost furnished the house, when he died of a heart attack.

Carl Porada, who had envied the possessor of that place every time he drove by it, had bought it, just as it was, as soon as he heard that some distant heirs of the unfortunate architect had put it up for sale. He had not consulted Alys. He was afraid that some other buyer might beat him to the purchase, and Alys was on a cruise with her mother, making up her mind whether or not to marry him. Carl thought that the house as tangible proof of his desire would settle that. He intended to surprise and delight her with a house ready for their occupancy when she came back. Instead he almost horrified her.

"This!" she exclaimed when she saw it. "Why, Carl, it's on the other edge of nowhere! What on earth got into you? And it's so odd-looking!"

"But that's it—that's why I like it. It isn't one of those places that you can never be sure is yours because there are so many like it in the same block."

"I wouldn't dare to be here alone—and you couldn't get any help—"

"That's another advantage. There's quite a Finnish settlement about a mile up the highway and you can get a woman from there for heavy work. I have one now who comes in to clean the place."

"But it's so lonely—"

"You have the dogs—they'd take good care of you and I'll never be any farther away than I have to be."

"Dogs always worry me—you never know what they're going to do—and they're a lot of bother."

Carl patted the head of one of the spaniels, who was bounding about with joy and admiration. "You can trust these fellows," he said, "and there might be a little more wild life in the house before too long to keep you company."

"Oh, Carl! Don't be coarse. Really, don't you see—I know you meant well—but don't you see this isn't the kind of house people have?"

"What people?" he asked, rather defiantly, to cover up the sickening disappointment.

"People like us. Why, everybody would think we were crazy."

"Why would they?"

"To live way out here. As if we had no friends. As if we were queer."

"Let's be queer then. Come, look it over inside before you begin to worry."

But the inside of the house pleased her no better. He showed her the massive built-in desk in the living room, the hand-woven multicolored rugs, the Danish chairs, the fireplace flanked by a huge copper kettle to hold wood, and old wrought-iron fire tools as tall as she was—he found himself explaining them, almost defending them before long.

Alys said, in the tone of one who was accustomed to getting what she wanted, "I just love French provincial—and everyone now has wall-to-wall carpeting. It makes a room so much more elegant."

"Really, Carl," she said when she saw the bed, "honestly! The man must have been a freak!"

The architect had put the bed in the master's room on a firm low dais—that would give a full lake view even when a person was lying on it—and it was a very large bed.

It was an hour that Carl Porada was not likely to forget. In the few weeks that he had owned the house he had already filled it with dreams, with shy expectations. He was a man who had not had much experience with women. Even now, although he no longer regretted Alys, she had shaken his faith in his house, spoiled his vision of it. He could see and hear her disdain out of the corner of his mind.

He told himself often now that the thing he should do was to sell the place and get a couple of rooms for himself in the city. The house was too big for one person. But he kept putting off the move because he was so busy and because of the dogs. Or because he did not want to let it go.

Alys had been a thoroughly disillusioning love. If she could not have found anyone who was richer and more tractable, she would have married Carl. He knew that. She hadn't let him go at once, in spite of the house.

She had tried light ridicule and coaxing.

She would tell him, "You wild man! What you really want is a wife who'll hitch up a covered wagon. You want somebody who'll go into the wilderness and make her own soap. And I'm terribly addicted to Germaine Monteil!"

Or, in quite a different and more dangerous mood, "Carl, don't you want to make me happy? You see, a girl wants to be near her friends, the people she's grown up with and has always known."

"My house is only fifteen or twenty minutes from the center of town."

"It's not just the physical distance, Carl," Alys would say reproachfully, as if he were unable to understand nuances.

Alys had also been critical of Carl's job. Her point was that if he wanted to be in politics, he should aim higher than a county job. Didn't he want to get anywhere?

"Why don't you try to get into the Senate, Carl? St. Paul and Minneapolis are wonderful socially."

"They're farther from your friends than the house out by the lake."

"But that's different. I was thinking of your future. And I have good friends in Minneapolis too, girls I knew at school."

She bewildered him and yet he was not fooled. When, during one of the reconciliations she seemed to need, he would hold her close and the perfume on her hair was the scent of temptation to do what she wanted, he would think that a man had to pay a price for this, and why not? But he held out about the house. He was determined, if they were married, to take her to the house he had bought for her, to try to make her happy there. If that was impossible, he would sell it. He told her that.

Then, on a holiday trip to Minneapolis, she had captivated a young widower who was already an executive in Honeywell. Carl had thrown his invitation to the wedding into the fire without a pang. Desire had gone out of him.

But her criticisms had stuck. He thought she was probably right about him. Not about the dogs. But about the fact that he wouldn't—probably it was couldn't—give a woman what she wanted. He was too stubborn. He wasn't ambitious enough. He didn't try to know the people who would help him to achieve higher positions and earn more money. She was right. He probably wouldn't get anywhere.

Carl had been thinking as he came back to his house through the storm tonight of how Alys would have hated the place on a wild night like this. He didn't hate it. It rather exhilarated him. He fed the beautiful spaniels and mixed himself a drink and told himself once more that it would be tough to give up the house but of course it didn't make sense to keep it. Nothing he was doing made sense. The county commissioner job was taking so much of his time that he couldn't expand or even keep up a good law practice. But now he was in so deep that he would have to run again for commissioner if he wanted to finish some of the things he had started. No one else would finish them.

At his desk before the window he opened his briefcase and drew out a sheaf of papers he had brought from the courthouse to study tonight. Sorting them, he found that he had shoved the note from that girl on the newspaper in among them. She certainly followed through, that girl. He read it again.

DEAR MR. PORADA:

You might like to know that the birth control clinic in the city does have a number of clients who are on relief. I was not able to get any exact figures on this, but I talked to Mrs. Angus Baird, who is the head of it, and she says that many of the women who come there for advice are on relief.

I want to tell you again how grateful I am for the help you gave me in connection with my piece for the paper, which will be in the Cosmopolitan section next Sunday.

Sincerely yours,
ANNE MILNER

She had obviously typed it herself and not on a very good typewriter. I wonder what she managed to dig up, thought Carl. If it's a good article—no, she wouldn't care what I thought. When she came into the office, I thought she didn't have a brain in her head. A girl like her, with a shape like hers, shouldn't go chasing around to some of those places. Things can happen. Of course it's the way she has to earn her living, but a girl like that won't have to earn it long. Some man will take over.

He moved his hand toward the wastebasket, then put the letter in a pigeonhole of the desk instead of discarding it. Vaguely he thought, she might have to get in touch with me again. The sleet beat fiercely against the huge window which surveyed the lake. He could not see it tonight, but he could hear the waves rage against the rocks. The sound was not disturbing. He thought, I suppose I am sort of a nut.

Francis Dearborn couldn't get any answer when he called Anne the first two times. But she was there when he telephoned at eight o'clock.

"Where on earth have you been?"

104

"I worked late. I was finishing that piece for the Cosmo section. It needed a little brushing and combing."

"Did you have trouble getting home?"

"It wasn't exactly a joy ride. The driving is dreadful."

"I've been worried," he said.

"You shouldn't have been. I made it all right."

"You take too many chances. We have to put a stop to it."

She laughed. "Chances are such fun."

"What are you doing now? Thinking about me?"

"I might just do that after I've satisfied hunger and thirst. Spend the evening in meditation on your charms, since we canceled out on dinner. I was sorry about that. There were a lot of things I wanted to talk about. One thing—do you happen to know a man called Porada?"

"Carl Porada? The one who's county commissioner?"

"That's the one."

"Yes, I know him. I was in law school when he was there. How did you happen to run into him?"

"I was on this assignment and went to see him at the courthouse."

"Why Porada?"

"This piece I've been working on is about relief—I was going to tell you about it, but I haven't had a chance because you've been out of town—whether relief is being exploited by unmarried mothers."

"For the Lord's sake, Anne, can't you keep off these subjects? First it's birth control—now this."

"I have to cover the assignments Max Fleming gives me. But tell me about Carl Porada. Do you like him?"

"He's a queer duck. Not too sound. He had a perfectly good spot with Lane and Webber, and he could have gone up in that firm. If he'd stuck to his knitting. Instead, he threw away the best chance a lawyer of his age could expect and went into politics. County politics at that."

"I suppose somebody has to."

"He didn't have to. He must have a little money—his father made quite a chunk. He was the owner of the Porada Tug Builders."

"I never heard of them."

"You wouldn't have. They sold out when the war was over and shipbuilding slowed down here. I think the old people went to Florida or California. Carl Porada stuck around. He's always been kind of a loner. I heard that he wanted to marry Alys Martin. She turned him down of course. He wasn't in her league."

She said, "I rather liked him. He was a lot of help when he got started."

"What do you mean—'got started'?"

"Nothing. He didn't approve of me at first, but then he warmed up."

"I don't like this. I don't like it at all, Anne."

"Don't like what?"

"Look, dear," said Francis, "you have to be careful. I think you ought to get out of that job before your name is connected with a lot of unsavory things."

"That's rather silly, Fran."

"I don't think it's silly at all. You can't touch pitch, you know . . ."

"Sometimes you have to," said Anne, "and you can always scrub up."

"I want to talk to you, Anne. I've been thinking about us. How about my coming over now?"

"You couldn't get up this hill tonight. It's a sheet of ice. Even the taxis can't make it. It was bad when I came in and it's getting worse all the time. I've been watching from my window. It's rather exciting. But I don't want you to break your neck."

"When am I going to see you?"

"Spring can't be far behind this weather!"

"Tomorrow night?"

106

"I promised Joyce I'd go out there for dinner."

"Can't you change that? Go some other night?"

"I don't know," said Anne doubtfully, "she made rather a point of my coming tomorrow. Chris is going to be out of town. Joyce seemed rather—I've been a little worried about her. I'll talk to her in the morning, then I'll let you know."

It had been a thoroughly disconcerting conversation, and when Francis put down the telephone he felt annoyed. She was safe at home. That much was all right. But the situation between him and Anne was getting out of hand. He felt the need for authority, the right to say what she should and should not do. She was becoming too independent. This job she had was going to her head.

She was going to be his wife and she should be thinking of that, considering how to build up her position in the city. His position. It wasn't going to help, a year or two from now, when he could afford it and managed to get proposed for membership in the Old Town Club, to have a wife who hobnobbed with everybody and who wrote stories for the papers on subjects that were either smut or pretty close to it. A girl who wrote about those things thought about them too.

It was not so bad when she was reporting social events, as she had been doing at first—but to go running around the courthouse was something else. Going to Carl Porada's office, thinking it was fine when he warmed up to her. He remembered Porada in the seminar—he was every professor's pet with his sure answer to a hard question. Francis remembered him, too, in the gymnasium, the tall figure placing a ball as easily as the legal answer. Porada was a flash in the pan, but he was smart.

After we're married, thought Francis, and was suddenly basking in the thought of that delightful, final possession. He would be better able to afford it if they waited for another year. At present he could invest a considerable part of his income, and his holdings were increasing in value. Here it cost him less to live than it would after he married. The old family house was paid for, the taxes were small and his mother was an experienced housekeeper. But he couldn't bring Anne here to live. She had said once that it would not be fair to his mother. And Francis thought that was true as well as sensible. With the money he could get from this house, he could buy a place in a good retirement home for his mother. He and Anne could start with an apartment, perhaps one in Mostly Towers. That was a very good address for a young couple.

He went back into the living room. His mother had finished washing the dishes and was tatting lace delicately, as her own Irish grandmother had taught her.

"It's a dreadful night out," she said.

"Fierce. I was just talking to Anne. She says her hill is a slippery slide—they can't get up it at all."

"But she is all right?"

"Oh yes."

"She should not be living alone like that."

"No."

"When are you two going to be married?"

"That has to be pretty carefully considered, Mother."

"Leave a thing too long on the fire and the flavor goes out of it," said Mrs. Dearborn. "Don't delay the dinner until you lose your appetite, my mother used to say. Your uncle John is a lonely old man in Dublin, and Stephen without chick or child in his flat in Boston."

"You needn't worry about my following their example," said Francis, "but marriage isn't something to rush into."

"Marriage should descend like the Holy Ghost," said Mrs. Dearborn, "in a flame."

The Hawley house always needed repairs, because something was always more urgent than fixing a shutter or putting a new drainpipe where one had rusted out. In fine weather such things went unnoticed, but in a storm like the one tonight the faults of the house cried out. Christopher Hawley was wakened by the banging of a shutter against the west wall of the house. There was nothing he could do about it now. He could not place or hold a ladder against the wall in the midst of wind and sleet. The shutter would have to blow back and forth, and by morning it would probably have fallen off and broken. He lay listening to the mischievous hammering and also heard the rush of water pouring down through the broken drainpipe. It would go down through the basement, for there was a crack somewhere, and he had meant to have a mason come and find it. There would probably be a flood in the furnace room again.

Luckily Joyce had not been awakened. After what she had told him tonight, he had insisted that she take two aspirins and a mild highball, and that had done the trick. She was sound asleep and he too had slept until now. The clock struck two. It was never right and he couldn't remember whether it was fast or slow, but it was about a quarter of an hour off. There was a long stretch until morning, and Christopher did not want to stay awake, because tomorrow he had to sell insurance and it was not easy to do that when a man felt like a dope. As he always did when he was short of sleep. He wanted to put what Joyce had told him out of his mind, to deny it for the time being, and he could not.

They were in for it again. Another one, and the bills weren't all paid for the last baby. She thought it happened that night last month after they had been to the football game. It could have. Joyce ought to keep better track of when it was safe. But they said there were some women you could hardly touch without making them pregnant. Funny, Joyce was so fragile—and all these kids.

A man wanted a family. Of course. He wouldn't part with one of them, not for all the money in the world. But another was a tough proposition. He had tried not to let Joyce see how he felt about this, and she was quite cheered up when he had said that maybe double-deckers in the boys' room would take care of all of them, and they could put a window at the end of the hall and screen off a place there for the baby. Joyce always felt better when there was a new plan for the house. But double-deckers and carpenters cost money, and the bills were rushing in the way the water was running down that broken drain. And that would cost money, too.

I ought to be gelded, Chris thought. I ought to be sterilized. The priests will tell you that you can't consider a thing like that. But the banks don't when you come in for a loan to get you through another of your wife's confinements. What do the priests know about it? They are fixed for life. They can get along without sex—most of them do, I guess.

It's one thing if a man has the money—if he knows that some grandfather will set up another million-dollar trust fund for every kid that comes along—and that his wife can have all the help she wants and maybe a trip to Europe for a change. And now Christmas will be coming up. I must talk to the kids—try to explain that Christmas this year is going to church and that's it. Not having presents would break Joyce's heart.

I have to get some sleep tonight. I'll be all in tomorrow. Hawley's losing his touch, they'll say behind my back. Handsome Hawley, who could sell insurance to anyone. I could, too —I could then. But the bills get you down and you need a drink and have one before you come home so you can be a little cheerful with your family, and then you have another that you probably don't need. It was probably whisky that started this kid on his way into a very tough world.

There's one good thing anyhow. We won't have to worry about that rhythm business for the next few months—we can have a little fun again. Christopher Hawley fell over the edge of his worries into an exhausted sleep.

Clare Baird got up from bed and went across the room to look out at the storm and see if it was as bad as it sounded.

When she drew back the heavy curtain, the wind rushed through a small opening at the bottom of the window as if it had been waiting for the chance. She pulled her soft robe closer and shivered. Violence had always appalled her.

Even the great Dutch elms were tossing about. There was the customary floodlight burning in the back of the garden at night to ward off or expose prowlers, and tonight it lit up the fury of nature. Branches had been torn loose, and sprawled on the ground. There was no sky, only blackness through which the rain was cruelly driven. She thought, excessive turbulence —that pilot told me it was almost the worst danger.

She said to herself, but where Angus is now it may not even be raining. It may be a moonlight night on the Pacific Ocean. Impossible to realize, when you look at this, that there's moonlight anywhere. He was vague about his schedule—as if he didn't care whether I knew where he would be or not. Always when he went away before, the itinerary was all typed out so that I could know where he was almost every hour. But not this time. He just said Herb had his schedule, would know where he was if there was any need to get in touch with him. If there was any need . . .

He was glad to get away. Horrible thought, but it's true. He wanted to take this trip and he never even suggested that I go with him. Would I have refused? I would have had to, if I wasn't going to cancel all those meetings where I've promised to make talks. But Angus didn't give me any chance to choose. That was his way of showing me that he wanted to put distance between us. To get away from embarrassment and humiliation and the person who's caused those things. Herb Martin said that's the worst of it, that Angus feels I've diminished him with the people who work with him and for him. Herb was certainly frank when he talked to me about resigning. He said that Angus didn't discuss it very much, but that it was obvious that he feels I've let him down terribly. It was odd, but in spite of what he said he thought I should do because of the

111

company, Herb seemed to understand how I felt better than Angus could.

Herb told me yesterday—poor Herb was embarrassed at having to be the one to tell me, but I had to find out, so I had to call him—that Angus will be in Colombia tomorrow morning. If their time is ahead of ours—is it?—he is there now and safe. As Clare tried to hold that reassurance close, there was a howl of wind, a crash, and sudden darkness on the grounds outside as one of the elms toppled over on the floodlight. Clare became rigid, unable to move for a minute. She was conscious of disaster—not the accident in her garden, but of peril somewhere over the sea—and of past tragedy, the wound from her parents' death torn open again in her mind.

Then a child cried out. She drew the curtains together and moved quickly to the light switch by the door. The room came back to color and luxury, the gold satin of the chaise glowing, the silver on her dressing table catching sparkles. Clare went down the hall to the nursery and picked up the startled child and held him close to comfort him.

"It's all right, Johnny. A tree blew down outside, and in the morning we must go and pick the poor tree up."

"Poor tree," repeated the child sleepily.

Poor all of us, thought Clare, laying him down again gently. When Angus went away like that, I felt like an outcast, though he was the one who was leaving. That cool kiss—the kiss for a nurse to see. He will soon begin to hate me, if he doesn't already. But I would rather have him hate me than come to my room as he did on that night two weeks go when he didn't like me or forgive me. Or even want me personally. He wanted a woman and had a right to one. That was the worst. He was ashamed of it in the morning—that was why he told Magda he had an early engagement and went away without breakfast. I was ashamed of it every minute.

In the dark again, in her restless bed, Clare tried to extend her thoughts, to find out what she had left out of them, to make

112

them complete no matter how they hurt. She did not spare herself the pain of thinking about what was lost. Of how often, so tenderly awakened and embraced, she had heard his voice as no other person had ever heard it, saying, "Oh my darling, I love you so much. . . ."

We were happier than other people. We knew it. We were always grateful for that. And humble, I think, because it wasn't anything we could take any credit for. We were fortunate. We were blessed. So many fine, good people—people who try very hard—aren't happy. Plenty of men and women desire each other, but for most of them the desire doesn't seem to penetrate—sort of illuminate everything in living together—the way it did for us. The look he would give at something I was wearing, and that was why I was wearing it—the telephone call that didn't amount to anything—suddenly realizing, as you looked at one of the children, that you and he had created that little person and that no other two in the world could have made that special child.

It was such fun. Most people don't have that much fun. We laughed at each other, but we didn't irritate each other—or because we could laugh, there was no irritation. He knew every fool habit I have—like going downstairs in the middle of the night if I knew there were some pistachio nuts on the coffee table and suddenly wanted them irresistibly. I used to tell him that he was Victorian because he was so sort of remote with me in public. When there were other people around, he never would touch me except to hold my coat or something like that. I was very much Mrs. Baird, and not the crazy girl he'd had in bed with him the night before. Angus is shy—and a little self-conscious with everyone except me. Except me! Now he's more self-conscious with me than with anyone else.

Please God he is safe tonight. Please God he is flying over a smooth, beautiful ocean in sunlight. I hope he's forgotten this trouble, forgotten me if that will do any good. If it will make him happy. Perhaps at this very moment he's going down to the lounge on the plane to have a New Orleans fizz before breakfast—the way we always did when we were starting off on a long vacation and felt hilarious.

How can I bear this for weeks—maybe months? He said he didn't know how long he would be gone. But it's better in some ways than living as we were. He knows I wouldn't hold him—I made the offer. There is no outlook for happiness—open one door and another closes. It's always worse at night. When the children are around I have to pretend, and that even helps me. For a few minutes I fool myself. And when I'm at the clinic and working, what I've done seems to have a reason, to make some sense again. It did the other day when I was talking to the Milner girl. Perhaps because she seems to be mixed up too.

Strange that a girl like that, with her job, should be a Catholic. Newspaper people are usually so crisp and disillusioned. Maybe that's why she isn't. She can't break away from it, she says. Lucky for her. I couldn't be a Catholic any more than my father could. But tonight I wish I could be. I wish I could believe that if I asked some saint in an unimaginable heaven to look after Angus and give him special protection and happiness, it would be done.

Chapter 9

❧❧❧

Angus Baird was flying without either a secretary or companion as far as Bogotá. Martin, the only man whose company he might have wanted, could not easily be spared from the home office at this time, for several new projects in the promotion department were under way and his experience was needed. He would have been reluctant to make the journey for some less obvious reason. There were other subordinates whom Angus might have taken with him, but he had agreed with Martin that this was not a trip which called for any parade of personnel.

Of course everything had been set up to make it useful. A man from the Baird Company's Brazilian branch, fluent in Spanish and expert in dealing with South American practices and prejudices, would fly from Rio to join Baird in Colombia, and from there the two men planned to travel the length of the western coast to Santiago. Their introductions were profuse and the arrangements detailed. At every stop a chauffeured car would be provided for Baird's use through the courtesy of that brother corporation, General Motors, and all the embassies had been informed by people in authority over them that an important American businessman was coming their way and that it was the part of wisdom to do all they could for him.

He had made the long flight to Panama yesterday, and by the time he was crossing the mountains in a local plane that shuttled from Buenaventura to Bogotá he had begun to feel detached from everything familiar. And when he traveled for pleasure Clare was always with him. Without her it was not a pleasure trip. So when it was sometimes impossible for her to travel far because of pregnancy or some need of one of the children, they would often spend a long or short holiday at the country place they owned on a river in Wisconsin. "In the woods," they would say, and there actually was a piece of a primeval forest surrounding the big, luxurious lodge. There Clare fished and hunted with Angus and guests who were stimulating and amusing. They both liked people and had a great spread of friendship and acquaintance, but since his marriage Angus had given up stag poker games and exclusively male parties.

In this flight over the Andes he was oppressed by the aching lack of his wife. He did not feel like his usual well-entrenched self without her to share a new view, a curiosity, an admiration. But to get away from Clare had been what he had told himself he must do. It was imperative. He had to think their situation through.

She had said one day, "Do you want a divorce, would that help?" He had answered coldly and conventionally, in spite of the shock of her question, that they had to consider the children. But none the less he did not know how long he was going to be able to endure the kind of life they had now, which was only an imitation of all that it used to be, plastered on top of his resentment and her resistance.

When he boarded the plane, Angus had taken a seat beside a window and opened a magazine at once, more or less as a defense against possibly having to talk to some of the people he had seen lined up at the gate. The plane obviously would be crowded to capacity, and there were a number of North

Americans who looked like the type who would introduce themselves and then pry for names and occupations and mutual acquaintances. Someone soon took the aisle seat beside him. Angus did not look up, but when the man leaned forward to put a small case under his seat, Angus moved to give the other more room and saw the Roman collar of a priest. Their eyes met, and with the briefest nod Angus resumed his reading.

The proximity of the priest was irritating. Another of them, thought Angus. They're everywhere, mixing into everything, pretending piety, but they stop at nothing. I suppose that down here they really have a strangle hold. Things that Angus had heard and read about the Catholic influence in South America and the way these priests exploited the people drifted through his mind. They wanted the natives to stay ignorant. To stay ignorant and to breed, so they could collect more money. What were those figures that had been in the papers last year about the size and management of the Catholic organization? It was one of the biggest, richest, smartest corporations in the world.

The plane reached cruising height. The priest was still and silent, but even that annoyed Angus. The presence of a Catholic prelate had torn open the whole miserable business again. This was one of the gang that had hounded Clare. He did not intend to take notice of the priest, but he was so angrily conscious of him that he turned his head involuntarily to see what the man looked like. He wore a crimson thing beneath the collar, so he was some higher-up. He was well past middle age. His face was gaunt and pallid and his eyes were closed.

Now he opened them as if awakened by that critical stare.

"Have I by any chance been snoring, sir?" he asked.

"Not at all," said Angus. The priest's voice was melodious and there was a hint of a chant in it. He had a slightly British accent.

"Weariness can snore upon the flint," said the priest with a smile, "or upon the plane. It's quite a long journey from Rome to Bogotá."

"You must be coming from your headquarters," said Angus. He had a sudden impulse, quite foreign to his usual reticence, to quarrel with this priest, to tell him what he thought about Catholic maneuvers and underground campaigns. He knew that he sounded curt and unfriendly and that was how he wanted to sound at the moment. He had been under control for weeks, but it was breaking.

"Some may call it that."

"I suppose you have to report in now and then. To Rome."

"If we are so fortunate as to be summoned, sir."

"All the orders come from Rome, don't they?"

The priest contemplated Angus before he spoke again. He did not answer the question. He asked, "Are you seeking to be informed or to confirm a prejudice?"

"I'm interested in the way your people do things."

"You will pardon me if I say that you seem rather hostile."

"I have every reason to be hostile to the Roman Catholic Church."

"Would you care to explain your reasons?"

"No," said Angus shortly. And then, "But why not?"

"Why not, indeed? It might be profitable for each of us."

"I doubt that. But I would like to know the answers to a few questions. My name is Angus Baird and I am a manufacturer in Twin Ports, Minnesota."

"That rarely beautiful city by the inland sea. I am Monsignor Lavas. My home is in the diocese of Bogotá."

The dignity with which he spoke and his manner reflected associations with which Angus was also familiar. This man had been about, had power and authority. He himself fell silent for a minute, unsure of how to proceed, wishing he'd kept his mouth shut.

"The questions you mentioned?"

"Well, one of them, Monsignor Lavas, is why your Church feels that it has a right to make rules for those who do not agree with its dogmas."

"The Church makes no such claim. It has no such right, of course."

"How about its attitude on birth control?"

"The Church does not assert or assume control over non-Catholic practices."

"I wish that were true."

"I assure you it is true."

"My personal experience proves otherwise," said Angus.

"I would be grateful to know what your personal experience has been to make you feel so convinced of something which has no basis in our theology. I am not moved by idle curiosity, Mr. Baird. But you have opened up a subject on which misunderstanding is so prevalent that it is causing many of my colleagues the greatest concern."

"I'll tell you exactly," said Angus. The story came easily now as he related it to this stranger beside him on top of the clouds. He told it chronologically, from the anonymous letters to the Board meeting, his subsequent information about chain letters, the facts about the falling off of sales. What he left out was only the agonizing impasse between Clare and himself, the bitterness which he would never expose to anyone but her.

"So that's why I feel, as you said, hostile to the Roman Catholic Church."

"It is a very shocking story," said Monsignor Lavas. "It illustrates both the ignorance and error that are often found in the lower levels of any organization. Do you not find such things in your own business at times? That some of those who work in your group misrepresent facts and policies?"

"If that happens, we fire them," said Angus.

"You have a certain advantage there," the priest said musingly, and for the first time in weeks Angus heard himself chuckle. Telling the whole thing had for some reason relaxed him. The man who listened so quietly and sympathetically had eased the tenseness of his nerves.

"Your wife must be a wonderful lady," said Monsignor Lavas. "It cannot have been easy for her to proceed as you say she has done."

Angus looked at the other man in astonishment. "But you don't approve of what she's doing. You're dead against it!"

"What you have told me shows the spiritual strength in her," said the priest, "truly admirable wherever one meets it. It is true that the methods of population control she advocates are not approved by my Church. Nor as yet have we found a common meeting ground. But let me make this clear. Catholic theology does not say—and Catholics should not be so taught, though sometimes this unfortunately happens—that regulation of fertility is contrary to the law of God or to the natural law."

"If that's true, what's the fight about? What's the shooting for?"

"To regulate the size of a Catholic family," said the priest, "two things are necessary. The reason must be licit. And the method must be licit. Which rules out artificial methods of preventing conception."

"That's the catch."

"That's the catch," agreed Monsignor Lavas with the smile which held a generous friendliness, "and a great many wise people are presently studying ways to release it."

"Even in Rome?"

"Indeed in Rome. And in South America. Here the majority of our clergy, Mr. Baird, are eager to accept a change in Church doctrine if it can be presented in an accepted moral framework."

"If . . ."

"Yes. It's conditional. But demographers all agree that we must face twin problems. One is population expansion, the other unwanted children."

Angus thought, Clare worries most about those unwanted children. She can't bear the thought of what they're up against —and once she told me that not thinking of them made her feel guilty.

"Believe me, Mr. Baird, the Catholic Church does not turn its back on the problems and adjustments of the modern world. To consider them was the reason why the Ecumenical Council was called."

"Everyone's read about that. It was a very dramatic setup from the pictures. But frankly, Monsignor Lavas, how far will it get? Will it get anywhere?"

"*La distance n'y fait rien—il y a le premier pas qui coute,*" the priest quoted.

"Maybe. Perhaps the first step is the most important thing. But I can't believe that distance doesn't matter."

"That was said of St. Denis. He walked two leagues, carrying his own head in his hands, according to legend."

Angus laughed aloud.

"It will get somewhere," said the Monsignor, "even if the delegates to the Council have to carry their heads in their hands. But I beg you to try to perceive the scope, the majesty, and also the delicacy of the problems it must consider. Such as this matter of birth control, which may, but probably will not, come before the present conclave. Nationalism is deeply involved, and makes great cleavage in opinion. You will find that here in South America the attitude of our clergy in Ecuador may differ from that in Chile, where there is great concern about the increase in illegal abortion. As a non-Catholic, you may also be interested to know that the Catholic hierarchy in the United States takes a far more conservative position on birth control than their colleagues in many countries on this continent and in Europe."

"Is that really a fact?"

"I assure you."

"Why is it?"

"Very probably because of the strong Irish influence on the North American Church. To revert to the unfortunate experiences which you have undergone because of your wife's activities—and convictions—I would venture a guess that what you have spoken of as the persecution of your wife and your business was instigated in various quarters by old or middle-aged clergy either born in Ireland or of Irish descent. They themselves were probably members of large families and idealized motherhood. I have met many such, admirable men and devoted priests, but convinced that God is in favor of the largest possible families. Ah, I feel the dip—we seem to be coming down. Are you remaining in Bogotá for some time?"

"Only a few days."

"You will see even in that short time that we have been discussing current social problems," said the priest, and he sighed as if resuming a burden. Suddenly his age showed and his weariness.

"This has been . . ." Angus began, and then said simply, "Thank you for talking to me, Monsignor Lavas."

The priest said, "It has been a pleasure, sir. If opportunity offers, you would be very welcome to call at the Bishop's residence. And should you regard our splendid cathedral, please bear in mind that it rises from the exact spot where Quesada built the first thatched church, calling it the Shrine of the Humble. I hope you will try to think of us with tolerance—we greatly need it. And allow me to send my respectful regards to your lady wife."

Chapter 10

~~~

The story in the Sunday *Observer* about county relief clients was well advertised in advance of its appearance in print, for Max Fleming, after he had looked it over, thought it might easily light a fuse which would lead to newsworthy political explosions. Also it bubbled over with human-interest facts, of the kind people liked to read in their Sunday papers when they had more time than usual. Hints of its contents were printed in boxes for several days to arouse curiosity, each one spicier than the one preceding it.

IS RELIEF NOW A WAY OF LIFE?
SUNDAY COSMOPOLITAN SECTION

HOW MUCH CHISELING ON COUNTY MONEY?
SUNDAY COSMOPOLITAN SECTION

THE TAXPAYER PAYS FOR IMMORALITY
SUNDAY COSMOPOLITAN SECTION

A BOUNTY ON ILLEGITIMACY?
SUNDAY COSMOPOLITAN SECTION

Anne's name was not used until the article finally appeared, but the advertising made her feel both embarrassed and defensive. She hoped that Francis would not notice those boxes, for she did not want to make an issue of this. Nor did he. When they had talked again after that unsatisfactory telephone conversation on the night of the storm, he had said that he did not want to discuss her assignments but that he was sure she understood how he felt about them. With that push, which was intended to send argument out of hearing, Francis was again the charming, devoted man who was binding their lives together with dinners and telephone calls and flowers and admiration, with expectancy that was very close to a claim. It was warming and exciting. After their impasse on that night Francis seemed more in love with her than he had ever been before. Anne seemed to hear it in his voice, even when it came over the long-distance wires. She was grateful. She told herself that she had been a little shrewish and rather mean in not fully explaining why she felt obliged to go to Joyce's house for dinner instead of spending that evening with him. Anne did not tell Francis that she had suggested to Joyce that she would like to bring him with her. But Joyce had said almost wildly, "Oh please don't, not tonight! Not tonight, Anne, I want to talk just to you."

Now Anne knew why and it was very troubling. Joyce's situation overshadowed her own work. It was mixed up with the things that Anne had been investigating and went along with her doubts. When for a few days recently Francis had been out of the city, she had missed him more than usual. It was not that she wanted to share her worry and concern for her sister, but she needed the feeling of reassurance that having a man who loved her close could give.

This was another Saturday night, and she had not wanted to go to any public place for dinner with him.

"Why don't you come up to my apartment? I'll cook something you'll like."

"That's too much work for you."

"No, it isn't. I love doing it. Let's say seven o'clock for the banquet."

"Shall I bring white wine or red?"

"Red will be wonderful." Francis liked red wines best, and so Anne bought two choice filets of beef.

She did enjoy preparing a dinner for him once in a while. To show how well she could do it, to surprise him with a minor talent. There was a kind of challenge to be especially feminine tonight. But she mocked herself for that as she arranged handwoven place mats on the gateleg table by the window, decided against a centerpiece of flowers as too commonplace, filled a copper bowl with bittersweet berries instead, and made everything ready in the kitchen so that there would be no flurry or confusion. The linen sheath she wore was almost the color of the glowing berries, simple and sleeveless, quite the right thing for a hostess who was also the cook.

She thought, still making fun of her own rising anticipation, in thousands of apartments girls are doing this tonight. Waiting for a man to arrive. For the first kiss, the cocktails with a special lift for some reason, the little dinner that will be so good because of being together and by ourselves. It's the dress rehearsal for marriage of course, at least it is that for Francis and me. Why shouldn't it always be just as much fun, just as exciting after marriage—will it be? Why can't it be if two people never take too much for granted, never get careless? Of course after a while it wouldn't be just two people probably—it would become more complicated. . . .

And Joyce came into her mind again, disturbingly. Joyce had declared the other night that she was very glad about having another child. But Anne wondered, underneath the assertion that she was happy, was Joyce defensive? It had almost seemed as if she were trying to be radiant, imitating the way she used to feel about her first babies. This was a blessing, she had said. Children grew up so fast. Anne had thought of Pearl Lemoy's saying the same thing and been aghast at feeling a reflection of Pearl's philosophy in her own sister. Something of the same attitude on sex? Of course not. A determination to believe that childbearing had precedence by right over everything else a woman could do? It was divine right with Joyce, that was the difference. Joyce was truly religious. She always felt—and had seemed, up to now—sanctified during her pregnancies.

But Anne hadn't been happy about this one. Nor about Christopher. Joyce had said that Chris was drinking too much. She told Anne that she was offering up a novena of prayers for a special intention, which was that Chris would cut down on liquor when he was on business trips. Anne had thought, it isn't a novena Chris needs so much as a few less worries and things to pay for. But she hadn't said that. She did not want to hurt Joyce. Nor had she said that she thought Sammy seemed pale and nervous and that the older children were getting a little out of hand. They needed discipline. But Joyce couldn't attend to everything. Anne thought now, Joyce adores Chris and the children, but she's exhausted about half the time. It isn't fair to them. Nor to herself. She's needed in so many directions that she's being torn to bits. And she used to be all in one lovely piece, so serene.

Is she pretending to be glad about having another child? Is she afraid because the last baby wasn't perfect? She says it's God's will. Is it His will or is it blind obedience—frightened obedience—to a theological doctrine taught by men who live in chastity and don't have ordinary domestic problems? I don't know. But before I marry—Francis and I must talk seriously about this. He puts me off when I try to talk about it. A maiden shouldn't write about birth control—or think about it. I won't bring it up tonight and spoil the evening. He will be here very soon. I must see if the lettuce is crisp. There's nothing worse than a limp salad.

Francis told her that the salad was perfect.

"You're a grand cook and a wonderful hostess. Tonight you're being your real self."

126

"Do you think so?"

"I know it," he said, and laid his hand on hers. She let it rest there. She thought, a man's hand can be so covering, so protective.

"You like me best when I'm domestic, don't you?"

"I would never want you to be too domestic. Certainly never a drudge. Just a beautiful all-woman."

"An all-purpose woman. A well-behaved rib, that's what you want me to be." She laughed, withdrew her hand very gently and said, "The crowning touch of this elegant meal is French Roquefort and coffee."

"I love you even more for the Roquefort. Most women would have settled for blue cheese."

She brought it to the table, and it was more than half an hour later before she said, "No, I'll wash the dishes later. I don't want men in my kitchen."

"Never?"

"Hardly ever. Not tonight. Will you move the table so that we can sit by the window?"

She poured brandy into liqueur glasses and they sat close, watching the lighted city, thinking of themselves.

"Anne, we're wasting time," he said.

"Everyone does on Saturday night."

"That's not what I mean and you know it. We should be like this—together every night. Married."

Anne said nothing in denial.

"When will you marry me?"

She gave a small sigh. "I don't know. There are so many things to consider."

"What besides ourselves?"

"Ourselves especially. But also your mother. My sister. And my job that you don't like."

"You don't have to give my mother a thought. She wants us to get married. There's nothing she'd like more. I'll find her a place in a good home for elderly people and she'll be fine.

127

And your sister has a husband of her own. Why do we have to consider her?"

"Joyce is having another baby. She'll need me to help out with things until that's over."

"Good Lord—another!"

"Yes. She says she's glad. But I think she's worried."

"About what?"

"Money, lebensraum. Her own strength. And whether another baby coming so soon after the last will be a healthy one."

"Those are problems that she and Chris Hawley have to face up to. You don't," Francis said.

"You said once that no one has any right to interfere with the size of anyone else's family. But it interferes with you if, like this, it's hard on someone you love very much."

"It's up to them, Anne. You have your own life to live."

She said, lightly enough, "You don't like the way I'm living it. And that's another thing to consider. My job."

"I've never objected to your having a job."

"I had to have one."

"And I've been proud of your work. I've always enjoyed your pieces in the paper—you have real talent, I think."

"You mean my wise and witty comments on the Junior League Follies?"

"You needn't laugh at them. That sort of thing can be very useful. It puts you in touch with people you want to know."

"Oh Fran, I want to know all sorts of people."

"I go along with that. So do I. I don't want to get stuck with any one group. But I want to know interesting, worthwhile people."

"The trouble is that I like people even when they aren't worthwhile. If I like them naturally. One of the most interesting women I've met in years is a completely immoral creature who is grateful that the various men she sleeps with never treat her cruel."

Francis Dearborn did not smile. He said, "A well-bred,

innocent girl like you is often curious about indecency. That's what sells all these nasty books."

"You think that's all it is, curiosity?"

"Let's not discuss it, dear. You know how I feel about your investigating such things. Let's forget it."

"We don't seem to be able to. I had the same idea, but the subject always pops up again. That's what worries me about us."

"You won't worry about us once we're married."

"It would be too late then. Much better to worry right now."

"Dear girl, don't you think I can take care of you?"

"What will we do about having children, Fran?"

"We'll figure that out at the proper time."

"We're both Catholics. We can't practice birth control."

He said, "I can understand why that's on your mind. Because of your sister. But you can trust me. I'll never get in Chris Hawley's spot. Nor let you get in hers."

"I don't see how you can be sure of that."

His chuckle was indulgent. "There are ways. I'm a good Catholic and I intend to stay in the Church and support it. But the size of my family is my own business."

Anne said, "There's rhythm—and there's continence. But they don't always work. Joyce has tried rhythm and you see. And I should think that continence . . . Nothing else is allowed."

"A great many Catholics don't take that seriously."

"Then they aren't Catholics, not really. Would you ever leave the Church?"

"Certainly not. It would kill my mother for one thing. And an apostate—people distrust a man who hops around from one religion to another. I was brought up to be a Catholic. But that doesn't mean it's necessary to be priest-ridden. Drop it, Anne, leave it to me. We'll decide when to have children.

129

Certainly if at first we should have an apartment in Mostly Towers—"

"Mostly Towers?"

"I can afford it. Even now. And next year the firm will give me a raise and, I hope, make me a full partner. That's far and away the best apartment house in the city. We wouldn't have to rent one of the penthouses. But what I was getting at was that in a small apartment we wouldn't have room for children. Besides, I want you to myself for a couple of years. When we have a house of our own—and that farm I promised you—we can begin to raise a family. As many as we can afford to educate and start in life as they should be started. No more. Now, does that put your mind at rest? Let's have some music. Shall I put on some records?"

She woke with a slight hangover and thought, it wasn't the wine or the brandy, it was the highball. Francis really plied me with liquor last night. He didn't want to go home—lucky for both of us that he lives with his mother. He is a good man. He doesn't go too far and he doesn't want to until we're married. But he goes quite far enough and I'll have to make it a matter of confession. It was a good evening. Fran had a very good time. He kept saying so.

I didn't promise. I told him I couldn't be married until after Joyce's baby comes, because while she's in the hospital I'll have to be available if they need me with the other children. It would save them quite a lot of money—the cost of good help to take care of that family would be wicked. Joyce thought it would be about the seventh of May—and I told Fran that June would be the soonest. I didn't promise a definite date, but that was why we had that final highball, the toast to next June—and surely everything will be in the clear by that time. It gives me time to think things out.

The telephone rang while she was in the shower and, wrapped quickly in a bath sheet, she expected to hear Francis say good morning. It was ten o'clock and he usually drove his mother to the half past ten service. I'll go to Mass at noon, and give myself plenty of time this morning, Anne decided on her way to the telephone.

"Hello!" She made her voice very wide-awake, with no hint of hangover.

"May I speak to Miss Anne Milner?"

"This is she. . . ."

"This is Carl Porada."

"Oh, how are you, Mr. Porada?"

"I feel fine after reading that piece of yours in the paper just now. . . ."

"I haven't seen it—I haven't gone down for my paper yet. Is it really all right?"

"It's excellent. It should start a lot of people thinking. And your paper certainly played it up. I've been noticing all the advance publicity. Got me a little scared as to what you might have written. But it's factual, not sensational."

"I'm terribly glad you think so! Thank you ever so much."

"I'm the lad to thank you."

"It wouldn't have been anything without those names you gave me."

"I'm surely glad I did."

"Well, thank you for calling—it certainly relieves my mind that you're not disappointed or anything. Thanks for calling," she repeated, eager now to see the paper herself.

He spoke quickly, "I called about the piece and also to ask a favor. It's sort of nervy of me and I suppose you're all tied up today, but the thing is that I'd like very much to talk to you for a few minutes sometime today. . . ."

"Today?"

"I know it's Sunday, but tomorrow's Monday," he said, and as Anne heard him laugh she remembered the boyish look on his face very distinctly. "It's that usual, extraordinary coincidence. And we have the weekly meeting of the county board

131

of commissioners on Monday. I'm going to propose something to them tomorrow that ties right in with what you wrote for the *Observer*. I thought it might interest you, and that maybe you'd give me your opinion as to whether it makes sense or would do any good. Also, I'd like to know how you think the people you interviewed might react to my idea. But I can understand that you probably wouldn't want to be bothered today. . . ."

"It wouldn't be a bother. . . ."

"Then could I drop by and see you? Make a little call and talk about this for a few minutes?"

"Why"—she was looking around at the room and thinking that it was one thing to have Francis here. But a stranger—"I just don't have callers here, Mr. Porada. I usually see people at the newspaper office—or I go to see them. I live at the top of this old house and—"

"Of course. I'm sorry. I guess I spoke out of turn. Well, anyway, let me tell you again that you wrote a good piece and I certainly congratulate you on it."

She felt foolish and ungracious and was quick to speak lest he break the connection. She had heard the embarrassed retreat in his voice.

"I'd like to talk to you very much, Mr. Porada. Not that I expect I'd be much help. I'll be free in the early part of the afternoon. . . ."

"Would you have lunch with me?"

"I'm just about to have breakfast."

"Or would you care to go for a little drive? It's a very handsome day. Half an hour is all I need to explain this business. I could stop for you any time you say, and I promise not to be a caller—"

"Oh, I didn't mean it that way."

"No reason why you shouldn't mean it. Naturally you don't invite every Tom, Dick and Harry who calls you up to come to your place."

She was thinking, I'm not meeting Fran until five o'clock at the Flame. And this man has been so decent to me. It's wonderful that he likes the piece. He must think that I'm utterly unsophisticated, a dreadful prude.

"I think a drive would be fine," she said. "I'd love to get out in the air."

"You would? Really?"

"Yes, how about two o'clock? The address is right there in the phone book, and don't let the house daunt you. If you'll ring me from what is laughingly called the lobby—the grim old vestibule—I'll be ready and come right down."

"You're being awfully generous."

"I'm being awfully curious," said Anne. "I want to hear what you intend to do tomorrow."

She thought that it might be an awkward meeting and planned to be so natural and relaxed that it would put him at ease. But that wasn't necessary. Carl Porada was completely forthright from the moment she met him. His manner made this an occasion which had an impersonal purpose. Anne herself had made no effort to be glamorous but was wearing her last year's plaid coat, which was shabby at the cuffs, and she carried a scarf to tie over her hair if it was windy. He helped her into the car, more or less at arm's length, took the other bucket seat and asked her, "Any special direction? Do you like the drive on top of the hill?"

"I like the North Shore better and there isn't much traffic at this time of the year."

"Right." He swung the car around. "I apologize once more for forcing myself on you like this. When you live alone, your manners don't get any exercise."

That answered one thing she had wanted to know and did not see how she could ask without seeming silly or over-conventional. He did not dwell on the apology but went on immediately, "I can put this thing pretty briefly and I hope

133

that you'll be perfectly honest with me. The reason I wanted to ask you about it is that there are very few people who understand what's going on and where it can lead. That's what gets me." He turned to look at her, his face stern with the problem, then faced the road again. "There's no foreseeable check on the growth of it, no end in sight unless something is done. You indicated that in your article. Not in so many words, but it came clear."

"It's true, I'm afraid."

"I'd like to give you a few figures," Carl Porada said. "I'll use round ones, because they're easier to carry in your head. The ones I'll give the commissioners will be exact, but these are close enough to give you the idea. The dependency program is only part of the relief load Dudley County has to carry—don't forget that—but in this county over two thousand children and about eight hundred mothers are supported by it. The federal and state governments pay about half and the county pays the other half."

"I know."

"You know more than I do after the way you dug into the situation. But anyway the monthly tab comes to approximately $127,000. In a year that amounts to almost a million and a half dollars."

"Heavens—I had no idea it was that much!"

"It is. Now I got the impression from what you wrote that you think a lot of these women take the line of least resistance. That they're more careless than vicious."

"I think that's true."

"And some of them have the sense and initiative to go after birth control information and help, but many of them don't. The clinic's too far uptown. The people who run it are strangers. They don't know what might be done to them or if they can get out if they don't like it."

"That's the way it is. They'd like to know how to keep from having more children, but they put it off. Maybe they haven't anything good enough to wear uptown. They hear talk about what treatment of that sort might do to them. Talk about old wives' tales—they're realistic compared to some of the things said about the clinic. And also some women think that going there is taking the path to hell. That's what they've been taught."

"I left that last out. Because as long as women feel that way, nothing can be done for them. But if others are just shy or lazy, or nervous about going to the clinic, why can't the information be taken to them? Into their own homes? This is what I have in mind. Suppose the county engages a competent nurse whose full-time job would be to circulate among these women, get their confidence and teach them how to take care of themselves—perhaps supply them with the things they'd have to use, or else tell them just where to get them and how available they are. You don't mind my being frank about this, do you?"

"Not a bit," said Anne. But she felt slightly hysterical with secret amusement as she suddenly imagined what Francis would say if he could hear this conversation between herself and a man whom she had met only once before.

"Here come more figures. A nurse's salary would be maybe five thousand a year. There are about two thousand children in the county supported while they're dependent. They grow up, but others take their place in line and it's an increasing number. We know that from the reports of the last two years. If this nurse were even a little effective—and due to her there were twenty less children for the public to support next year—she'd save the county more than it pays her. If there were a hundred less children out of that two thousand, she'd save the county twenty thousand dollars. And it might be better than that."

"But it's not just the money. . . ."

"I know that. I'm using the money angle for all it's worth, for that's what might put the idea over with the commissioners and the voters. But I know a lot of those kids should never be born—for their own sakes."

She was silent with thought. They were approaching the city limits now, and the shore road stretched its length along the lake, winter-bleak and beautiful.

"Do you think the idea has any merit?"

"You told me that day in your office that you didn't like the idea of sterilization."

"There wouldn't be sterilization. Just explaining prevention."

"Many people don't make the distinction—they think there's no difference. Or that one thing inevitably leads to another."

"Of course the Catholics will put up a howl," he said cheerfully.

"I'm a Catholic," said Anne.

He turned his head toward her again, slowed the car a little. His glance was astonished. Rather dismayed.

"I didn't know that. I would never have guessed it. That piece you wrote didn't seem to object to birth control."

"I was reporting. I was on a job. I had to give the facts. The *Observer* didn't take a stand."

"I see. But under the circumstances I suppose you personally wouldn't approve my plan?"

She said, "Suppose your nurse does teach these women how to keep from getting pregnant. It won't make them decent women if they aren't that, and if they aren't, some of them may even sink a little lower, for having a child gives them a kind of usefulness and a little self-respect. Take Pearl Lemoy. . . ."

"God, that Lemoy bunch is a headache—two generations now."

"Just the same, there's something about her that's kind—I liked her—and she's apparently good to her children."

"One of those boys is already headed for trouble."

"Luke?"

"You've got it all taped. You're thorough. I think that's the name. He came up in juvenile court and they called my office to find out what the status of the family was."

"Poor Luke."

Carl Porada asked, as if his mind had gone on to something else, "Are you a practicing Catholic?"

"Yes, for what that ridiculous word is worth."

"Then I've really put my foot in it. You'd be against the county hiring a nurse whose specialty was birth control."

"There are plenty of non-Catholic women she could work with."

"That's an evasion I can't understand. If the thing is right for women who aren't Catholic, why isn't it right for all of them?"

"Catholics have a different attitude toward life than other people," said Anne rather laboriously. She sounded depressed.

"This has disturbed you. That was the last thing I wanted to do. I'm very sorry."

"There's nothing for you to be sorry about. But it's not a very exhilarating situation."

"You'd tell me not to suggest this nurse?"

"Would it make any difference if I did?"

He seemed to consider that. Then said, "I think I have to go through with it. I hoped, you know, that you'd be on my side."

She did not answer.

"Do you want to turn back to town?"

"If you like."

"I don't like," he said. "I'd like to drive a bit farther and talk about something else."

"Let's do that," said Anne, "now that we understand that we don't understand each other."

"I'm not so sure of that. Anyway, I'm glad that you wanted some fresh air this afternoon. So did I."

"We're getting it," she said, and knotted her scarf and rolled down her window a little more.

"It's a wicked old lake in winter," he said, "but always something to look at, isn't it?"

"I love it at any time of year. All times."

"I was brought up on it more or less. To me it's like a relative. My father built tugboats and always owned one. He was a master sailor. Have you ever been on a tug?"

"No, but I watch them from my window. They're very competent. Are they fun?"

"They're not pleasure boats. But you have a good time on them. They're very dependable, that's the main thing. Brave little cruisers. They can stand right up to a storm and take it when other craft can't."

"As that house just ahead on the left that sits there all by itself must have to stand up to storms and take them," she said.

His eyes went toward the house they were approaching and the speed of the car slackened.

"What do you think of that house?" he asked.

"It's one of my favorites. When I drive past it I always envy the people who live there. Someone does. There are dogs. I've seen them."

"What kind of people would live there, do you suppose?"

"Certainly the kind that aren't dependent on neighbors," said Anne, "and don't want to talk over the back fence. Or borrow things. Pretty self-sufficient people—they'd have to be that. They'd love beauty or they wouldn't live there. Think of what it must be like to wake up to this view in the morning!"

"I suppose someone might like the place," he said dubiously, regarding his home.

"Don't you?"

"I did when I first saw it," said Carl Porada, "but I don't know. One thing is sure—people who lived in that house would have to go along together, see things the same way."

138

"Oh yes, it would be horrible if they didn't—impossible in a place like this."

"Quite impossible," he said, speeding up the car and obviously losing interest in the house. He was silent for the next mile and then said, "I'm afraid I've spoiled your Sunday. I hope you'll believe that I wouldn't have telephoned you this morning if I'd known . . ." He left that unfinished, with a frown at his clumsiness.

She thought, he's guarded and afraid to talk now because I'm a Catholic.

"You didn't spoil my Sunday. I had nothing to do this afternoon and it's been a lovely drive. But I think I should go back now."

He made a U-turn immediately. They went into their separate thoughts for a long distance. Then Anne tried to tie up the loose ends.

"If you really care to know what I think about your project," she told him, "I believe it's worth trying. But you would have to find the right kind of nurse. She would have to be very wise, very tolerant, not in the least bigoted—and sympathetic with people who don't believe in birth control."

"She'd have to be all of those things."

"If you put this over—if it comes to anything—why don't you ask Mrs. Angus Baird to help you find the right person?"

"You think she would?"

"I'm sure she would. She believes just as you do," Anne said, and she herself felt left out, which was absurd. Resisting that, she went on, "I'll be watching the papers to see how it comes out. One thing I would like to ask—aren't you afraid it will do you harm politically to propose this?"

"It certainly will do something to me politically." He laughed as if that excited him and said, "Probably harm, possibly good. That's the chance I have to take, and what of it? If I believe I'm on the right track."

She thought of what Francis Dearborn had said to her

about this man. And wanted to find out something else about him. She asked, "Why did you go into politics?"

"There were a good many reasons. You get uneasy about things. You can't keep your mind off what seem to you to be blunders and cheating. I suppose the main reason was that in politics there is a chance of direct action. You can steer a thing in the direction you think it ought to go—try to, at least."

"That's the tugboat in you," said Anne.

"Could be! You're sharp—you're wonderful. You see right through me. But I like it better than loading cargo on some big hulk of a freight boat and that's the job of an underling in a law office. That's what I was until three years ago."

"You wouldn't have had to stay an underling, would you? You might even have become captain of the hulk some day."

"It can be pretty stuffy at the top," said Carl Porada.

Chapter 11

❧❧❧

During the ten years of their marriage Clare and Angus Baird had made the Christmas season a time of beauty and delight in their home, building up small special habits and traditions, perfecting decorations that were more loved each time they were used. On their first Christmas in the house there was already an infant in the nursery. Now Angus, Third, familiarly known as Gus, was nine. Susan was eight, Mary four, and John was learning to walk. And, though no one else remembered him now, Clare never forgot her second boy, who had lived only an hour and to whom they meant to give her father's name, Philip. At Christmas she hung an invisible stocking for him too by the fireplace.

Cars almost always slowed in admiration as they passed the Baird house after the twentieth of December. Two tall spruce trees on either side of the driveway glowed with hundreds of lights, and even from the street the row of golden angels could be seen within the windows of the second-floor balcony. The gleaming tree in the drawing room might also be glimpsed, for the curtains were never drawn at night during the Christmas season.

The angels were one of the traditions. Angus had given Clare one, a fragile, exquisitely made figurine of crystal and gold, on that first Christmas, and she had loved it so much that every year he searched for other angels. She had a collection of them now. The Swedish ones, made of gold-colored straw, stood on the ledges of the staircase, and one with a singularly beautiful face held a vase with calla lilies on a table in the entrance hall.

The tree in the drawing room was exquisitely trimmed with white, silver and glass ornaments. But there was also a children's tree in the lower library, properly garish and confused, which revolved and sang carols. The children themselves trimmed that one and strung popcorn and cranberries to hang in festoons from its branches. Clare wove into the holidays more than costly decorations. The children were allowed to stir the batter of the Christmas fruitcake, excitedly believing the legend that any secret wish mixed into it would be granted. Susan had an Advent calendar and opened a shutter on each day. Every year on Christmas Eve Clare read aloud the story of the Nativity to the ones who were old enough to understand it. They all, even John, joined in singing carols before they opened their presents. To delay our greed, Clare would say.

On Christmas night, although no invitations were sent out, there was hospitality in the Baird house. Close friends usually came to admire the tree and exclaim again over the rare beauty of the angels and drink Irish coffee or eggnog. Herbert Martin had always been one of that company. But this year he had not known what to do, whether he should come to see Clare or stay away from her. This year everything was different.

He did not know what Clare would do about celebrating Christmas, with Angus still in South America and with trouble between them. Better than any other of their friends, Martin understood how serious the trouble had been and he knew that it was not yet over. He had not been in the Baird house since Angus had gone away. Clare had called him several times to get information about her husband, and though she sounded cool and poised, Herbert Martin knew that to do it must have shamed her. It embarrassed him when Angus wrote or cabled about his movements and occasionally added *Please inform Clare*, proving that he was not in direct communication with his wife.

Martin had never permitted himself longings or dreams that he knew could not be satisfied. He had been a close witness to the tenderness between the Bairds. He had never doubted the depth of the passion which he did not see. But Clare was always deep in his consciousness, the reason why he was as he was. During the recent struggle he had felt in it with them, supporting Angus as he must, yet wanting secretly, instinctively, to take Clare's part.

As Christmas drew near, his thoughts of Clare had become more definite and disturbing. The Bairds had made such a thing of Christmas that he knew Clare must be suffering from remembrances—lacks and contrasts. He could not make up his mind on this Christmas night whether it would be harder for Clare to have him go to her house or stay away from it. Finally he decided that he would drive by the Bairds' house. If the house was dark, or dimly and unhappily lighted, he would not intrude on her.

The Baird townhouse was in a district where only the wealthy could afford to live. Martin drove by the huge stone mansion of the Ginns, recalling that they always had that same scene of the Nativity on their lawn, behind a high and forbidding iron fence, which cast unpleasant shadows on the colored plaster figures. Some of the other houses had flood-lights on flights of reindeer or a life-size Santa Claus on their roofs, showing that children were in residence. Some were almost dark except for small gleams from quarters occupied by caretakers, for their owners had already sought milder climates for the winter. Martin found himself vaguely hoping—knowing that it wasn't important but hoping none the less—that the Baird house would not be dark. He turned the corner from which it would be visible and came upon its brilliance. She had done everything just as usual. He braked his car across the street, for an automobile was coming out of the driveway. It passed and he could see no other cars near the house. Clare would be alone. Martin waited irresolutely, looking at the tall, lighted trees, but the desire to see her grew stronger.

There were no servants on duty. She opened the door herself, and there were relief and pleasure in her voice as she said, "Oh, I'm so glad—so glad it's you, Herb! Come in. Merry Christmas."

She was wearing a garnet-colored hostess gown that gave her a queenly look and the lights in the hall were muted, so at first Martin thought only that she was more beautiful than ever. She led the way into the drawing room, where a fire glowed at one end of the room and the white-trimmed tree sparkled at the other.

"Your tree is as beautiful as always," he said.

"Let's sit by the fire," said Clare, without looking at the tree. "Irish coffee? It won't take me a minute. I just made some for the Reynoldses—they were here. Just left."

"They passed me. I didn't know who they were."

"I don't think anyone else will come along. Thank goodness."

"You're tired? I won't stay—don't bother with the drink."

"Oh please, I want you to stay. But with them—and there were a few others—it's so difficult to pretend. With you I don't have to."

She busied herself with the silver kettle and the decanter, and now Martin saw the utter lack of gaiety, of happiness in her face. She mixed two glasses and he set them on a table and moved a chair for her close to it.

"I suppose the kids are exhausted."

144

"Oh yes, they fell into bed. They had a wonderful day. Have you heard anything more from Angus?"

"Not since I talked to you the other day. He'll be in Santiago all next week—too bad he couldn't be home for Christmas."

"He didn't want to be home for Christmas," said Clare, "and he was right. I was very glad he didn't come. I don't think I could have gone through with all the—you know, the trimming and the singing and the rest of it—if he had been here. Much better not."

"He's doing a grand job down there."

"It's going well?"

"Far better than we expected. He's sure that we can open up new and very profitable markets in several countries. It will mean the biggest expansion we've ever made in the corporation if it comes off."

"That's good," she said, "that's fine. Will it make up for the damage I've done to the company?"

"It will more than make up for it—two or three times and better than that."

"You're giving me a very fine Christmas present, Herb."

"I'd like to. I've been so sorry about the whole mess, Clare. But the thing is blowing over, I believe. My guess is that somebody called off the dogs. Some higher-up in the Catholic Church. I don't know that, and if it is true, nobody is ever going to admit it. But it could be true. Things are easier. Sales are picking up again. I wouldn't be surprised if we are back to normal in the next quarter."

"Good," she said, but drearily.

"And another thing," said Martin. "Those letters are falling off. There are a few but not nearly so many."

"I didn't mind the letters too much. But Angus did."

"He hated to have you the target for a bunch of nuts."

She said thoughtfully, "There was much more to it than that." And in the same reflective, frank way, Clare went on,

"Herb, before Angus went to South America I offered to give him a divorce."

"You did? A divorce?"

"Yes. I asked him if he wanted one. I thought it might be the best thing."

"But he didn't think so?"

"I don't know. He said that we had to think of the children. But I'm not sure that he doesn't want a divorce, even if he doesn't yet admit it to himself. Or to me. I know that he wanted to get away from me, that our life together was becoming unbearable. Worse all the time. When he comes back, I'm going to talk about divorce again with him. Very seriously. As far as the children are concerned, it would be better for them to have it over while they're too young to be badly hurt."

"But Clare, I've just told you that the situation is much better. Clearing up."

"For the company. But not for Angus and me. You don't know what I did to Angus and to our marriage."

"I believe you exaggerate that."

"No—I shamed him. I disgraced him. He's very proud, you know. Reticent—almost shy about us. And I exposed him. This wasn't a private disagreement. It was public. A great many people know that I refused to do what he asked me to do."

"Angus has always had things too much his own way, that's what is the matter with him," said Martin in a voice that was suddenly hard.

She did not seem to notice that. She said, "You told me I humiliated him—you knew better than anyone how he felt."

"Maybe it was good for him," said Martin in the same tone.

"It was very bad for him. He was proud of our marriage—we both were—we thought it was better, stronger, than most marriages, more beautiful. And now he can't be proud any more. So it's impossible to live together. He will always be conscious that I failed him. As of course I did."

Martin said, "He'll come around. He knows he can't get along without you. This South American trip will give him a chance to think things out, get some perspective. He's made things very hard for you."

"I had it coming to me."

"No, you didn't. And I blame myself to some extent, Clare. I was the one who approached Angus in the first place and suggested that he ask you to resign. I didn't know that the thing meant so much to you, was so important to you."

"Not just to me. But I couldn't resign."

"I'm glad now that you didn't. That you wouldn't knuckle under to old Ginn. Or anyone else. I admire you for it. And so do a good many other men on that Board of Directors."

"But not the chairman," she said quietly.

Martin had been staring at the fire as he talked. Now he turned to face her. He said in an anger suddenly released from great depths in himself, long smoldering and suddenly blazing, "Good God, you gave him everything. A home, children, your love! You were utterly devoted to him—no woman was ever more faithful! But that wasn't enough for Angus. He wanted that little piece of your mind and conviction and energy that you'd given to something you believe and that you couldn't surrender to Angus if you tried!"

"You knew that," she said in astonishment. "When you argued with me, I felt that you knew—"

"I knew. I should have come out and said so. But I was Angus's man. And he had to show who was boss, to show his Board that he only had to tell his wife what to do and she'd do it. You talk about his being proud—it's his damned ego!"

"Why, Herb—you're his friend!"

"I've tried to be. I have been his friend. But, Clare, you must know how I feel about you. Don't you? You must know that I love you—I have loved you for years. When you spoke of getting a divorce a few minutes ago, the whole world lit up for me—I rejoiced in my bones—because all of a sudden there was just a chance—"

"Don't!" said Clare. "Don't say anything more. I have just realized how fond I am of you, how deeply fond, how close—don't spoil that, Herb. Please go now—go away so that you can come back."

Chapter 12

❧❧❧

Angus Baird got out of his car and instantly, as if they had been bred that moment in the pavement, a swarm of little boys who seemed made of wire and elastic bounced around him, begging. They were children whose eyes, gleaming in the lights set on the locked gate of the residence of Señor Luis Martinez, were wild and sly. Angus had seen such children in all the countries he had visited recently. They gave no feeling of having come out of homes. They were undersized, too thin, uncannily quick.

The chauffeur brushed them away with the gesture of a whip and rang a bell. The wooden gate, which was as large as a small wall, swung open and a servant bowed to Angus and conducted him through a courtyard with a cobbled floor into a large inner court where a fountain was playing. The house it fronted had the old, sure beauty acquired by generations of fine living, and the manners of Señor Martinez as he greeted his guest of honor had the same patina.

He was the Minister of Trade, and the invitation to dine with him proved—as did the other guests whom Angus met in the tall, cool rooms—that there was much interest in what the Baird Company might wish to do in Santiago. Señor Martinez regretted the absence of his wife. She was in Paris. "Our ladies must seasonally attend their dressmakers," he explained indulgently.

No women were present. But the Minister had gathered together a mixture of important men. One was from the American Legation, and there were several Chilean businessmen, the head of the British Trade Mission, whom Angus had met in Ecuador some weeks before, the president of the largest bank in the city, about whom Angus had been briefed by his own man from Rio, and a Chilean introduced as a doctor. Presumably a physician, thought Angus, using his trained social and business skill to identify each man. There was also a priest. "My nephew, Father Juan, who teaches in the Catholic university and edits also a most philosophical journal," said Señor Martinez in his careful, heavily accented English. Angus was becoming used to the presence of priests. He saw them on the streets, their black robes swinging through the crowds, in the hotels, at the races, even in the Jockey Club in Rio. This one was a young man who kept himself a little apart and in silence during the serving of the apéritifs, but he had a fiery, eager glance.

Dinner, served at ten o'clock, proceeded formally for the first hour. Then the conversation, warmed by several wines, moved toward inquiry and opinion. Angus was seated at the right of his host, with the Chilean banker, who understood English better than he could speak it and occasionally lapsed into French, on his other side. Lord Brandon, of the British Trade Mission, faced him across the table. The Jesuit was seated at the far end, but the company numbered only ten, and if a subject commanded general attention, all the others could hear what anyone at the table was saying.

"Your company, it is all belonging to your family, yes?" asked Señor Martinez.

"Oh no, Señor Martinez," said Angus, "it belongs to the stockholders and we have many of them. The firm carries my family's name because my grandfather started it. He was a farmer and raised more food than he could sell when it was ready to eat. Then he got the idea of canning the surplus so it wouldn't spoil. That was eighty years ago and since then the business has grown considerably. Today we still can some vegetables—and most of our baby foods are canned—but we also package mixes. You know what we call mixes are?"

"Surely—the mixes. No cooks now in North America."

"Cause and effect," said Angus with a smile. They were all listening to him now.

"Your company wishes to locate a tinnery in Chile, yes?" asked his host.

"I don't know, sir. I wouldn't go so far as to say we do at this time. That is a matter which would have to be decided by our board of directors."

"*Les directeurs, mais oui*," murmured the banker beside him, nodding in agreement.

"I came down to South America," said Angus, "at their suggestion. To see what the possibilities are, and to be advised by gentlemen like yourself. We would like to know if our company would be welcome, if our products would be useful so that there would be a market for them. For example, if you need our baby foods—which, by the way, are used by many invalids and old people also."

"Very remarkable products," said Lord Brandon, "extensively used in Australia."

"Food is always needed," said Señor Martinez. "We have large populations in South American countries. Getting more large all the time, yes? This creates problems of seriousness."

"A problem that has to be solved," said the doctor. He was a shrunken, almost untidy man, and his black tie was a little askew. But as he spoke they all looked at him with interest and respect. The banker leaned forward and said something in rapid Spanish. Angus could understand only a few words. The doctor answered the comment in Spanish, but then, obviously realizing that Angus would not know the gist of the conversation, he turned to him and spoke English faultlessly.

"Señor Labarca says that we have the solution. He refers

151

to the antifertility pill. Chile has had a committee studying the methods of population control, because we have been concerned about the increase of illegal abortion. But the difficulty is to get the people who most need it to use it. Its use is hampered or neglected by ignorance, forgetfulness, passion, wines and"—he addressed the young priest with the greatest courtesy—"by the objections of the Church, Father Juan."

"The Church is not unaware of the need for population control," said the Jesuit. "It is no doubt the central human problem in almost every country in the world. But the Church cannot give its communicants permission to break the natural law."

Angus remembered that on the plane Monsignor Lavas had spoken of the same thing. He asked, "Will you be kind enough to explain what you mean by the natural law, sir?"

"The natural law," the priest replied, "is placed in man by God so that his human activity may direct him to that perfection which is proper and possible to his human nature. In the case of the reproductive powers, God has designed them quite obviously for the purpose of procreation. These powers may fail or be unused without sin. But the use of an artificial method like this pill to prevent procreation is an infraction of the law which God, in creating man, has made part of him."

"However, the consequences of not breaking the law," said the doctor, "are increasing starvation and misery. A starving man or homeless child does not commonly achieve perfection."

Angus thought of that clutching crew of boys outside the gate of this house, where erudite explanation of doctrines concerning their existence was offered over lavish food and beautiful silver.

"I hope very much, Mr. Baird," the doctor continued, "that your company does come here and make a great deal of baby food for us. I am sure we shall have better nourished Chilean children in the class that can afford to buy your foods. But our overpopulation is among the very poor. We used to have epidemics—they had some deterrent effect on the natural law, Father Juan. But we are conquering disease to some extent and repressing wars. The thinning-out process is being checked and that creates the hideous overcrowding that exists in many places. Whether our conquests over plagues and wars are for the common good may be questioned if one is cynical enough."

"But the consequences of breaking the natural law," answered the priest, with a conviction that seemed indifferent to argument, "are worse than even starvation and misery. Life becomes worthless. It is held in contempt, rejected by men and women. So abortion, which is murder—far worse than murder, for it denies baptism to a living being—then becomes commonplace. No society can sanction murder without corrupting itself." He relapsed into silence, which hung over them for a few seconds.

Lord Brandon broke it. "Doctor, you say that it is difficult to get ignorant people to make use of the pill. I have heard the same comment in many countries in Asia. Also in Africa. What would you suggest as a solution?"

The doctor said, "I believe we must come to vaccination against fertility. Establish limits on breeding by law. Have vaccination that will be effective for a period of years enforced by governments as yellow fever and smallpox were controlled by such means. If inoculation is required by authority, people fall in line. And governments will eventually see that the control of fertility is more important to them than expanding markets or trips to the moon. It must be the primary concern of modern civilization."

Angus Baird thought, Clare would go along with that last remark. She said to me one night, "Of course I'm heartsick about hurting your business. But this thing I'm working for is more important than the sales of the Baird Company."

Señor Martinez brought the talk to a personal level.

"You must tell me more about these remarkable foods for

children, Mr. Baird. Also it would interest my wife. We have six children. All now have marry. Me, I have nineteen grandchildren, perhaps no more children. My wife, she says she does not feel like a nineteen grandmother. Ha! We shall see. . . ." He laughed sensuously as some memories or anticipations evidently slid into his mind.

"You have a family, Mr. Baird?"

"I have four children."

"Little ones, yes?"

"The oldest is nine." Angus picked up his glass of brandy.

And Gus was in the Country-Day school, where Angus himself had gone when he was that age. Gus would be going off to school this morning—it would be morning there—no, he wouldn't, because it would still be the Christmas vacation and both Gus and Susan would be home. Last year during the midyear holiday he and Clare had taken the older children down to the lodge on the river. The snow was very deep but well crusted, and Gus began to handle himself pretty well on skis. He would be a natural athlete. They had followed animal tracks—deer, ferrets, and a wolf one day. Clare wouldn't take them down there by herself of course—or would she? She loved the place in winter—always had. It had a special feeling after the snow came. Short days, bright or maybe snowing, and long evenings before the fire with a few drinks and a game of gin rummy. Making love was wonderful on those cold nights—all the warmth was yourselves but, as she said, that was plenty. Oh God, why did Clare have to ruin it all? I couldn't have done anything else. Christmas must have been hell for her this year. But she had the kids. It couldn't have been as bad for her as it was for me. I got plastered and stayed that way for two days. I haven't done that in years, since long before we were married.

That was what he thought as he sipped the brandy and lit a cigarette. He wished this man would get off the subject of families.

154

"So your wife cannot leave the little ones. . . ."

"No. She's at home."

"Well—what you say? Absence makes the heart more fond. . . ."

It wouldn't. When he had left that day, Clare had been cold as ice. She had hardened up. She was withdrawn. If she had cared, she wouldn't have let him go like that. She would have come to the door, out to the car. . . .

Angus turned from Señor Martinez to brave the banker's English. He asked about construction costs in Santiago.

It was a successful occasion. Angus was quite sure of that, recognizing many small signs which indicated that Señor Martinez would be favorably inclined when the Baird Company got down to doing business. If it did. He was beginning to formulate a plan, but the Board might buck him. Under the circumstances, with sales not what they had been, he couldn't count on anything.

The good nights were cordial and he accepted an invitation to lunch with the banker. But Angus was glad when the time came for him to leave. Only the priest and the doctor were still there. Angus had told his driver not to return, that it would be simpler to call a taxi to take him back to the hotel. But Señor Martinez would have none of that.

"Ah, by no means—Father Juan will take you in my car."

"Allow me," said Doctor Salas. "You are at the Crillon. I pass it on my way home."

Angus thanked him, preferring the doctor's company to that of the Jesuit. The car was parked in the courtyard, and the great gate was unlocked and swung open by a servant. They could hear it click again under a key as the doctor turned into the street.

"They have to keep well locked apparently," said Angus.

"Vagabonds—did you notice when you arrived?"

"Yes. They've all gone home now."

"Home," the doctor repeated and shook his head. "Most of

them have no homes. Those are the ones who should not be born. They will steal, do small evils, then larger ones. Worse, they will breed."

"I was interested in your remarks about that at dinner," said Angus and added, though he did not know why, "My wife should have heard them. She's involved in the birth control organization in the States."

"Is she, indeed? That gives you a great deal in common. Both of you working to improve the fate of children."

"I hardly think of myself in that light."

"You must be interested in nutrition."

"Of course. We employ quite a staff of dieticians and some others who do nothing but research to improve our foods. It's always been our policy. And it pays off. Kids really thrive on our stuff, if you'll forgive a little boasting."

"A statement of accomplishment is not boasting." He stopped the car suddenly on the side of the road. They were driving through one of the city's parks and the doctor opened his door and got out to look at something. Angus saw a small figure on the ground—was there more than one?

Doctor Salas came back and started the motor. "Just asleep. A couple of boys. But I wanted to make sure they were not dead. Excuse me, please."

"Are they allowed to sleep there?"

"They are allowed nothing. But the police are often not unkind."

"Are there many of those poor kids?"

"There will be more," said the doctor. "Mr. Baird, I very much hope you succeed in your project to manufacture food for children in our country. But there could not be enough baby food made or adult food made to satisfy hunger at the rate we are breeding. And this is what we call a white country. In Ecuador and Peru conditions are worse because of the Indians."

"And the Church blocks what you want to do, from what you said to the priest tonight."

"We are all Catholics," said the doctor. "I hope we did not confuse you with our family argument."

"Is that what it was?" They both laughed. The doctor stopped his car before the Crillon.

The doorman came to attention. But Angus said, "I'm not going in just yet. I want to walk a bit."

Chapter 13

❦❦❦

Max Fleming's trained nose for news had been able to smell the political controversy latent in the relief situation. But even he had not anticipated that it would be such a hot one. He had not known of course that Carl Porada would go to the mat as he did and definitely propose taking birth control information and aid to all women on relief who wanted it. Not that it be cautiously and half secretly permitted but that at least one nurse be openly employed and paid with county money to take the information to them. That would be her only job, and the results would be closely watched and measured for statistical purposes.

It was one of the most drastic proposals that had been made on the problem that was simmering all through the country, and soon eyes from many directions were trained on the actions and attitudes of Dudley County. The news magazine *Future* carried an article about it, with the description:

This is a normally conservative county, which went Democratic by a narrow margin in 1960, and has a large though not preponderant Catholic population, of Irish, German and Polish descent. The largest city in the county is the historic Fond Port, terminus of the Great Lakes.

Bishop Bolles sighed as he read about it. Father Collins prayed for restraint, but he could not in conscience leave it alone. And he thundered on the Sunday after Carl Porada laid his plan before the commissioners, "There are enemies in our midst, enemies of all moral values, enemies of the family and the home. It is not only permissible to protest, by ballot and other influence, the suggestions that human beings be deliberately persuaded to tamper with the sources of life—it is our duty as Catholics to openly oppose it. My dear people, not long ago I watched a mother die in childbirth. I anointed her, I held her hand, I told her and her sorrowing husband to rejoice that she had brought another soul into the world. She smiled. I believe she did rejoice and I know that the angels received that woman." The thunder in his voice hushed to devotion as he finished, and several parishioners wept.

There were other reactions. The legislature was in session at the Capitol, and in one of the cloakroom sessions where more went on than did on the floor of the Senate, the thing came up.

"I saw an item in *Future* about the impact that a fellow named Porada is making in Dudley County. That's next door to your district, Sam. Do you know Porada?"

Sam said, "I've seen him around. He's young. Pretty unlicked. Looks like an astronaut. He's got a very hot potato in this birth control for people on relief."

"Not so hot as it used to be. Looks that way, but maybe Porada's nobody's fool. He probably knows that a whole lot of people who won't say so are on his side. I'd be inclined to believe he isn't doing himself any harm. At any rate he's getting a hell of a lot of free publicity. What's his party?"

"He ran nonpartisan. Independent, as far as I know."

"Would he by any chance be a replacement for Lobel up there? Even Lobel must know that he has to bow out after this term. That trachoma is a killer. Lobel can't even read the titles on the bills any more. We could use a brainy young fellow from that neck of the woods—someone who isn't afraid of the cars."

Letters poured into the *Observer* office intended for the daily column called "The Mail Bag," which printed letters of opinion from readers of the newspaper. A statement at the top of the column said that personal attacks would not be printed, and anonymous letters were never used. But signatures would be withheld if the writer of a letter so requested.

One member of the staff had the job of selecting the letters that could be used in the limited space that was available, choosing those which were the most intelligent, or most original, or sometimes most absurd, to give the public a laugh. The job was a heavy one after the Porada plan was put before the county commission. There were letters sent to "The Mail Bag" during the winter weeks which the newspaper would not have dared to print a few years previously. But suddenly the lid was off. Not only was the subject of birth control no longer taboo, but there was mention of methods. Opinions which had been kept under wraps for years suddenly were having their day in the press, and if attacks on Porada were not quite to be classified as personal, many letters made it clear as to who was under their fire.

That day the editor of "The Mail Bag" decided on printing one which was signed "Happy Mother of Six" (Mrs. Ralph Dulane—do not use my name). Also one signed H. D. Raley, retired welfare worker, which analyzed what was being done in North Carolina without public protests. That balanced emotion with statistics, and the editor himself was interested in the letter from the traveler back from Japan, which said that Japan's method of birth control through legalized abortion had resulted in that country's finding itself with too many old people and a possible shortage of young ones, with parents unwilling to have more than a couple of children and the nation needing more productive people.

"Damned if you do and damned if you don't," said the

editor to the man at the next desk, and decided to confuse the public with the statements about Japan. He opened another letter.

"Here's a honey," he said. "Look who's here. Monogrammed paper, address on the Heights. Cecilia Ginn—could that be *the* Ginn?"

"Better ask Anne. She would know."

Anne read the letter that "The Mail Bag" editor showed her.

She said, "Yes, that would be Mrs. Lucius Ginn. It must be." The letter read:

DEAR SIR:

There are many ways in which life in our community could be contaminated. The water supply could be poisoned by carelessness in disposal of filth. A single typhoid carrier could infect hundreds of healthy people. The air we breathe may some day be laden with fallout from hydrogen bombs. But none of these contaminations is to be compared with the danger inherent in one recently suggested to the officials of Dudley County. This one would poison the morals of the community. It would seep through the walls of our homes. It would bring death, slowly or suddenly, to thousands of souls. As a citizen for many years, as one who has tried to be of service in bringing beauty to this city and to the region, and as one who believes that God cannot be mocked without certain punishment of those who do mock Him, I enter my protest against this immoral and evil proposal to teach unfortunate women how to destroy life.

Sincerely,
A CATHOLIC CITIZEN

(Cecilia Ginn. I do not want my name to be used.)

"If she feels that strongly about it, I should think she wouldn't be afraid to stand up and be counted," said "The Mail Bag" editor. "But I suppose I better print the opinion of the aristocracy. How many children does she have?"

Anne said, "There's one granddaughter that I know of,"

161

and went back to her work. She was maintaining a poker face about the whole thing. She was out of it now, but she read all that was printed, the arguments in the commissioners' session, the usually sidestepping opinions of citizens who were interviewed. Pictures of Carl Porada in the newspapers had been frequent. He was very photogenic, she thought. The pictures were action ones—he didn't pose—but the photographers caught him bringing down his fist in determination, and once a television camera had caught him laughing at some question.

"Your friend Porada seems to have got himself out on a limb," said Francis Dearborn.

"My friend?"

"I thought you took quite an interest in him. You went up to the courthouse to see him, you said."

"That hardly makes him a friend. Though I wouldn't mind if he was. Why do you say he's on a limb?"

"This nutty idea of his."

"Oh that—I don't think it's so nutty." She hesitated. Be honest, she thought. Don't make a thing of it—there was nothing to it anyhow. "As a matter of fact, he told me that he was going to propose that."

"How did that happen?"

"I don't know. I suppose he knew I was interested because I did that other job."

"Did you see him after that?"

"It takes a lawyer!" exclaimed Anne, and then laughed. "Well, yes, if I'm on the witness stand, I saw him again."

"You haven't been going out with that fellow?"

"I wouldn't call it that," said Anne. "I don't believe it could be built up to that."

"I don't think it's so funny."

"It wasn't funny. It was quite serious. Sorry, Fran dear, but I hate to be badgered. Actually he telephoned me because he wanted to get my opinion of this proposition before he made it. And we went for a ride in his car and talked it over for an hour or so. And didn't agree too well."

"Why a ride?"

"Because I didn't want to ask him up to the apartment. He isn't that much of a friend! And I couldn't see him at dinner because I was having that with you. And it was just the day before his meeting. Therefore the ride."

"But Anne—look, dear, I know you have this yen to be free and do just as you please. You unmanageable girl, I suppose it's one of the reasons I'm so crazy about you—a man likes to be teased up to a point, but there's a limit. You must use some sense. Going around with Carl Porada—especially when he's on a hot spot and mixed up in things that are turning over a lot of stomachs—could get you involved."

"I haven't been going around with Carl Porada," Anne said.

"Well, don't make any mistake about it," Francis said, almost sharply. Then, not liking the expression on her face, he changed his tone to affectionate persuasion. He said, "Just suppose some news photographer snapped a picture of you with him. And he has those people following him around right now. He encourages it because he's trying to make hay for himself, get his name before as large a public as possible. Obviously he's a sensation hunter."

"I don't think so. I don't care—but I think you're wrong."

"If he isn't, he lacks judgment. Anyone with balance would know that a politician can't afford to get mixed up with a deal that touches on religion or tampers with accepted morals."

"He knows it's dangerous. He said so. He said he was willing to take a chance on its doing him harm."

"Martyr stuff. He fed you that—"

"No—oh what are we arguing about him for!"

"That's what I say. No more arguments tonight," Francis said, "that's my girl."

And she was his girl for the next hour. They took their martinis slowly and, as always, it was wonderful when they didn't argue.

It was on the six o'clock television broadcast of local news. Anne had turned on the little portable set in her kitchen when she came in tonight, more interested in the weather report than what else might be happening. But as she broke the eggs for the omelet that was to be her supper, she saw the boy held by two policemen on the screen. He seemed vaguely familiar. He had a fancy hairdo, ridiculous because the stiffness of the duckbill was not in the right place. His head was held defiantly, and his insolent, half-lidded eyes stared straight at Anne. As before somewhere. She could almost see him walk. It looked like—yes it was, they were telling the story now. It was Luke Lemoy.

He was twelve years old, the broadcaster said. Anne remembered that he had looked older than that when she saw him on the street, but that would be his actual age, according to the relief records. He had gone home with a switchblade knife, presumably doped, attacked his mother and then tried to kill his half sister. A half brother had come in and Luke had then run for it. But he did not get far. The local police knew the boy well, for he was a persistent truant and window-breaker, and, alerted by the half brother, two officers had caught him.

"The mother, who is pregnant," said the broadcaster, "is not expected to live."

"Oh no—no—" said Anne.

"The sister is in serious condition. Interrogated as to the reason for his outbreak, the boy said, 'I don't like women.' He will be held for juvenile court, in the detention section of the jail, and probably undergo psychiatric examination."

The voice began to report traffic accidents, and Anne turned it off. She stirred the eggs, flipped the omelet and went on getting her supper. It was horrible, and there was nothing she could do about it. Poor, friendly, loose-living Pearl Lemoy deserved better than that—than death at a child's hands. She liked children, brought them into the world without complaint. She had said, "The truant officer is awful down on Luke." She didn't blame Luke.

And that wild child must have hated her, thought Anne. Hated his mother and his sister. "I don't like women," he had said. It meant that sex—what he had seen and heard in that house—had revolted him. And some drug loosed all restraints and someone said something—or again he saw something—and he pulled the knife.

Anne wondered if Francis had seen that on television. Probably. His mother kept the set on most of the time. I'd like to talk to him about it—no, if I told him that I knew the woman, it would just bother him and he'd say I shouldn't know that sort of person. No, I won't call him. I'd rather not talk to him tonight. I don't want to talk to anybody. The thing is so sickening. I might drive over there and see if there's anything to do for those children. I wonder how Carl Porada will feel about this. He'll remember—he spoke to me about the Lemoys—and he knew that boy was running wild.

She tried to think of something else, but her mind was disobedient. It came back to the Lemoys. It went on to Carl Porada. What would he say? Would this be useful to him or not? Luke was a boy who should not have been born. Well, why shouldn't I, she asked herself, almost angrily. She picked up the telephone book.

"Yes," said Carl Porada, "I know about it. It's a very bad business."

"It seems to prove what you've been trying to tell people—that poor kids like that shouldn't be born."

"He'll need a lot of help. If he can be straightened out at all. And that won't bring the poor old girl back to life, though she didn't have much but her sins to live for. I'm glad the sister is going to come through."

165

"How about the others? The young ones? Who takes over?"

"I don't know. I suppose at the moment there are neighbors. I thought I'd take a run out and see for myself later on this evening. Shall I call you and let you know how things are?"

"Yes, please. Unless—would it be all right if I went there with you?"

There was a pause. Then Carl Porada said, "I don't know why not, Anne," as easily as if he always had used her first name.

Chapter 14

❧❧❧

Morris Street had been dreary and unkempt when Anne had first seen it in the daytime. Tonight it seemed ominous, as if vice and uncontrolled passions might be lurking in the black shadows between the ugly little houses. There was only one feeble streetlight at a distance of several hundred feet from the house where the Lemoys lived, and as Carl Porada and Anne left his car they heard the slap of water in the harbor against the stony edge of the vacant lot at the end of the road.

Carl was carrying two large grocery bags, for Anne had said they must not come here empty-handed and that the children would need food. So they found a supermarket which stayed open in the evening. Anne had chosen fruit, canned meat, cinnamon rolls, butter and jam, piling high the little wagon that Carl pushed around the market. It was a strange thing to be doing and once, for a minute or two, Anne had found herself involuntarily enjoying it as if it were adventure. She squashed the feeling like an intrusive bug.

He would not let her pay for anything. "No, that's my end of it," he told her with authority.

Another car was parked in front of the house with the broken numerals beside the rusty letter box. The penciled message that the bell did not ring was still there. A tall, very tense boy opened the door for them. Anne guessed that he must be Rex, the legitimate son of the murdered woman. The girl with the bandages around her chest who lay on the lumpy sofa was of course Jenny. A young man wearing a black pullover sat beside her and his serious expression seemed to indicate that he had been comforting or advising her. The baby was asleep in the playpen, and when other children began to clamber down the rickety stairs to see who had arrived, Jenny raised her head and said sternly, "I told you kids to go to bed," and they disappeared.

Carl put the brown paper bags down on a table.

"I'm Carl Porada," he said, "and this is Miss Milner. You're the young lady who was hurt?"

"Yes," said Jenny. The married matron of seventeen did not have the seductive beauty of her mother. But her thin face was well modeled and Anne thought that normally the girl would have style and spirit.

Jenny asked, "Are you from the police?"

"No. I work for the county," said Carl Porada.

"Oh, you're the welfare."

"I'm connected with it. We brought a few things for you and the children to lunch on tomorrow."

"I'm very much obliged."

"I was sorry to hear of your trouble," he said quietly and Anne was surprised at the skill with which he seemed to be putting the girl at ease. "Shouldn't you be in the hospital?"

"I wanted to stay with the baby," said Jenny, "and the kids. The doctor said I could if I don't move around too much."

Carl looked at the young man in the black sweater. "Are you a relative?"

Rex Lemoy suddenly laughed aloud.

"No. I'm the priest in this parish. Father Walker."

"I beg your pardon—"

"No need," said Father Walker with a smile, "you gave Rex a laugh and that's good. I had my work clothes on because I was patching the roof on my house near here—and when I heard about this I came over just as I was."

"You've been wonderful, Father," said Jenny. Anne remembered that Pearl Lemoy had said that Jenny was religious and she heard the reverence in the girl's voice. "Father Walker is going to try to help Luke. Explain to the police that he didn't know what he was doing. He gets in these rages, and then if he thinks he has it in for somebody . . ."

"Don't talk about it now, Jenny," said Father Walker. He was regarding Carl Porada with interest, measuring him with a very keen glance. He said, "You must be Commissioner Porada."

"That's right, Father."

And so you two are enemies, thought Anne. On different sides of an insurmountable fence, for Carl is publicly demanding something that no priest will allow. What has happened here today proves that Carl is right—Pearl Lemoy shouldn't have gone on having children. But Jenny will do what Father Walker tells her to do—or, if she doesn't, she will believe that she should—and I'm in the same boat. . . .

"May I have a word with you, Mr. Porada? Perhaps if we stepped outside for a few minutes? Jenny should be quiet."

Anne carried the grocery bags into the next room, which she remembered was the kitchen and put away the food, then came back to Jenny.

"I know my way around a little because I was here one day to visit with your mother."

"You're the lady from the newspaper?"

"Yes."

"Mom liked you. She said you were nice. She said you were a Catholic too."

"I am."

"Father Walker is wonderful. The priest we had before

him at St. John's—he was kind of cross. I suppose I shouldn't say that about a priest."

"Why not? They often are cross."

"Father Walker never is. He understands about things. You see what happened—Luke had it in for me and Rex. Because—well, Rex and I are real brother and sister, and Luke—I guess he was jealous or something. So he was always trying to show off, to show that he didn't have to mind anybody—he'd skip school—but then sometimes he'd be just as nice, real sweet with the baby. Oh my God, this afternoon I thought he'd go after the baby next, he was so wild. Poor Mom. If Rex hadn't come . . ."

Rex, stiff and silent against the frame of the door since that one laugh, said, "Skip it, Jen. They told you to."

"Your mother was very proud of you, Jenny," said Anne, "she liked to talk about you and what you were doing."

"She never had it very good," said Jenny, and tears began to trickle down her cheeks. She brushed them off with a crumpled tissue. "But Mom was never mean to any of us. That's what will come over Luke when he makes sense and gets the dope out of him. It'll just about kill him too, but he won't ever admit it."

Carl Porada and the priest came back into the room. Carl left it to the priest to talk.

"Jenny, do you think you and Rex can make out by yourselves tonight?"

"Oh sure," said Jenny, "mine's just superficial, that's what the doctor said. He's coming again in the morning."

"In the morning I'll send over the woman who takes care of my house to help out here," said Father Walker. "That's on me, Jenny. She won't expect you to give her anything. And don't worry about Luke—he's probably asleep by now. He's being looked after. I'll offer my morning Mass for your mother, children." He paused, then asked, "Would you like me to bless this house?"

"Bless it? Would you?" breathed Jenny softly.

"I will, indeed." He picked up his overcoat and felt in its inside pocket, bringing out a flask. "I always carry a little holy water with me for emergency baptisms—or accidents."

This wretched place can be blessed now, with Pearl Lemoy gone, thought Anne and knelt down beside the couch. With a quick glance at her, Rex also slid down on his knees. Carl Porada retreated to the farthest corner of the room while the priest flung holy water in both directions, spoke a few sentences in Latin and gave the benediction. He had just finished when there was a knock at the door. Rex opened it and they all stared at two men crowding the narrow doorway, one of them with a camera slung over his shoulder.

The other said, "This the Lemoy place? We'd like to get a picture for the *Daily News*."

Porada, near the door, instantly took over, easing Rex to one side and blocking the men from entrance as he confronted them.

"No pictures, boys. There's illness here."

"Well—Commissioner," said the newspaper man in a surprised voice, "I suppose this ties in—"

"No comment," said Carl Porada and spoke to the others over his shoulder. "Let's go. Rex, lock up after we're gone. And stay locked. Coming, Father?"

He let the priest pass him first, still guarding the doorway. Then Anne.

"Turn your head," Porada told her. But she was not quick enough. The flash of the camera covered both Anne and himself.

They hurried to his car, and speeding away, Porada cursed the newspaper men, then laughed.

"But I suppose they're your pals."

"That's not my paper. Don't blame me for that pair."

"They may not have caught you and me with the camera. Anyway, it's better for them to have a picture of us than one of those poor kids in that shack."

"I was so glad that you wouldn't let them in!"

"It would have been sort of an anticlimax, wouldn't it? After the priest had gone through his little ceremony. Is that customary?"

"Some people like to have it done. When my sister and her husband built their house, they had it blessed."

"What's the theory of it?"

"It's what is called a sacramental. Like blessing throats to prevent diseases of the throat."

"You can't take that seriously, Anne?"

"I don't have to. Sacramentals aren't required. But it was good to have him do that tonight for the Lemoys. It made them feel protected. Didn't you think so?"

"It seemed to mean more to the girl than the groceries," said Carl. "That priest is a good man."

"Do you think he can help Luke?"

"It's hard to say. That's what he wanted to talk to me about when we went outside. The boy's a murderer. He can't be let off. But he's a juvenile and a mentally disturbed one, probably. The priest thought that since the family is on relief, Luke is a ward of the county and that I might have a little influence in seeing that he's treated as a sick child instead of a degenerate."

"Will you?"

"For what it's worth," said Carl Porada. "Whatever is done with Luke will cost the taxpayers a lot of money, and the chances are that he'll always be way off beat. I put it right up to the priest tonight. I said, 'Look here, Father, this is a case in point. If that wretched woman had been made incapable of bearing children, she'd be alive today and we wouldn't have a murderous boy on our hands.'"

After a silent moment Anne asked, "And what did he say?"

"Oh, he was very civil. He said that he could understand why a tragedy like this might seem to prove that wrong was right, but that the conclusion was fallacious. He speaks the King's English. He said that the situation was extremely complicated and a lot of thought was being given to it. Then he said that pity for individual deterioration could not justify support of mass deterioration. He sort of beat around the bush, but he didn't do any backing down on being against birth control for these miserable women."

"Carl, the priests don't want those women to have children they can't take care of any more than you do."

"Then why in hell—" He stopped and said, "I shouldn't take it out on you, should I?" and drove her home.

He took her key and unlocked the door of the vestibule of the old house, stepped inside and looked around it.

"Is it comfortable here?"

"I have a little roost up at the top that suits me fine."

Carl Porada said, "Remember that house you liked on the lake shore—when we were driving that Sunday—off by itself?"

"Yes—that enchanting place."

"That's mine. That's where I live."

"Honestly?"

"Yes. I'll probably sell it."

"Why? Don't you like it?"

"The girl I bought it for didn't like it at all."

Anne remembered that Francis had told her that Carl Porada had wanted to marry a girl. "Who wasn't in his league," Francis had said.

"More fool she," said Anne.

"No, it was more fool me," he said and still lingered.

"Will you tell me something? Answer a very impudent question?"

"I might. What is the question?"

"Someone told me that you were Francis Dearborn's girl. Is that true?"

"I'm very fond of Fran."

"Are you two thinking of getting married?"

"We've thought about it a great deal," said Anne.

"Dearborn's clever," said Carl Porada, "you'll never starve, that's sure. And he's your kind too, isn't he? A Catholic, I mean."

"Yes, he's a Catholic."

"So you'll see eye to eye on everything. Well, that's good for a marriage."

"But we—" began Anne, and stopped. No, she said to herself firmly. If we don't see eye to eye, that's between Fran and me.

"Well, good night, Carl," she said, "and thank you for taking me along. I'll sleep better than I might have."

"Good night," said Carl. "I admire you, Anne. You have what it takes. That and a lot more." Bending from his height, he kissed her. "Dearborn can spare that much. Is that all right?"

She did not know the answer, and as the door closed Anne went slowly up the stairs, wondering.

Chapter 15

✦✦✦

"It was not my original intention," said Angus Baird to his board of directors, "to make such an extensive survey or to be away from my job here for so long a time. But as those of you who are familiar with South America know, the tempo of doing business down there is different from ours."

"Three hours for lunch and wines with each course and then everybody has to take a nap," said Clyde Ferris. "I know. I've been there."

"Didn't seem to put any weight on you, Angus," said Solomon Frank.

He looks very well, thought Herbert Martin. He is thinner but more relaxed. I thought he'd be fit to be tied when he came home and found Clare wasn't there. When I called up to give her word of his arrival and heard she was off on this planned-parenthood speaking tour, I was sure there would be trouble. But Angus seems to be handling himself much better. Is it because he's made up his mind? Perhaps he feels as she told me she does, that they can't go along together, and is calmer because he's made the decision.

"And it's not just the tempo," Angus was saying, "but each country has to be considered by itself. Especially for our purpose. It would be one thing for us to set up an operation in Chile—which calls itself a white country and where we would be intelligently welcomed—and quite another thing to do business in Ecuador, where the population is so heavily weighted with Indians and we'd have a job of educating the public. I had these little outline maps struck off to give us a base for discussion. There's one in front of each of you. I've marked in red the places where I think we could make a start, where we'd probably have good markets and co-operation."

"Anything like this would involve a great deal of capital outlay," said Funston Smith. "Where's the money going to come from? We don't want to reduce our dividend. We mustn't bite off more than we can chew."

"It would take a lot of money," agreed Angus.

"But you think it would pay off?" asked Solomon Frank. "Is that your opinion, Angus?"

"If we do it right, I think so. In fact, I'm convinced that it would."

"I've had a hunch that we were missing a bet in not covering more areas of South America," muttered Peter Daniels, studying the map before him. "This is very interesting. You certainly got around, Angus."

"One thing led to another," said the chairman.

"But as we just heard from Mr. Sanders, our sales are improving. Do we need to take the risks involved in any expansion at this time?" asked Kingsley Jones.

"I was very glad to hear that the sales have perked up," said Angus to Charley Sanders. "What's the explanation for it?"

"Well—the new packaging helps. It's attractive. And when the women try other things, they usually come back to our products after a while."

"Are we still being boycotted?" inquired Angus.

"Not to any great extent. The wind went out of that. I think it may have been called off by sensible higher-ups."

"Always was a tempest in a teapot. Silly business," growled Daniels.

Mr. Ginn spoke. "With that I cannot agree, Mr. Daniels. As a matter of fact I know that harm was done to the prestige of the corporation. I know that many people are still disturbed by the continued association of the Baird name with this so-called planned parenthood. And the situation has been aggravated by the tawdry proposition of a politician, which is spread all over our papers. I still believe that it is not only to our financial interest, but necessary to maintaining our standing in the community, that we should disassociate the names of any persons whom the public connects with the corporation from matters which should decently be private and not public affairs."

Angus Baird had listened with complete and courteous attention, although some of the others around the table did not try to conceal impatience or boredom as the pompous phrases rolled off the old man's tongue. When he had finished, their eyes went toward Angus. This was up to him. She was his wife. And they all had heard that there was trouble between the Bairds.

He left a little gap between the challenge and his answer. Then he said very calmly, "Mr. Ginn, I do not think that position is sound. It may have been defendable in the past, but it is not today. The pressure of population is certainly not a private affair. Wherever I traveled recently I found it a topic of discussion. It is a matter of the greatest concern to the clergy, doctors, businessmen—and they make no bones about it. I have been told on very good authority that it is discussed in Rome at high levels in the Catholic Church. If the problems it involves can be considered frankly in Rome, I don't see why we should sweep them under the rug in Fond Port. I am not at all apologetic for my wife's participation in the birth control movement—I assume that was the implication of your critical remarks. If I may say so, I have come to take considerable pride in her activities in this field."

If she could hear him, thought Herbert Martin in amazement. And with an involuntary wave of dismay. Now there was no use in hoarding that bit of hope. He thought, I didn't think Angus had it in him. He's learned a lot somewhere, somehow. He's a stronger man. And he's made it up to her.

"But I want to make one thing clear to this Board," Angus went on. "If at any time Mr. Ginn's fears should prove to be well founded, and the financial interests or the honorable reputation of this company should be damaged seriously and permanently by the activities of any member of my family—or by my own for that matter—I shall immediately resign both as chairman and as director. I have said 'seriously and permanently' because all corporations have their ups and downs and go through flurries of more or less popularity with the public. But you have that assurance."

The bright red spots which had appeared on Mr. Ginn's thin-skinned old face were the stigmata of inner fury.

He said, "Mr. Chairman and gentlemen, I believe that serious and permanent damage already has been done to this corporation, and that all of us have been enforcedly allied with antisocial and un-Christian propaganda and action. Personally I would be willing to consider the chairman's offer to resign at this time."

Solomon Frank's composed voice invaded an astonished silence.

"I think no other member of the Board would consider it," he said, and his eyes roamed gravely around the table, counting the unspoken vote.

It will be Mr. Ginn who will have to resign, thought Martin. If he doesn't have a stroke first. He's lost so much face that he can hardly stay on with any dignity. Not one of the Board would back him up, not even Kingsley Jones, who usually lets Mr. Ginn push him around because he wants big Ginn subscriptions for his causes. Peter Daniels is having a field day. He can hardly keep his face straight. Some day perhaps I shall tell Clare about this reaction. Angus will never tell her.

In Chicago all the planes were grounded. For Clare Baird it added confusion to her weariness. She had slept very little during the last week. But she had gone on doing what she had promised to do, keeping all the engagements that the organization had booked for her. Dayton, Des Moines, Cedar Rapids blurred in her mind. They were a succession of dinners, luncheons and platforms. Of saying the same things over and over again, and trying to keep persuasion and feeling from leaking out of what she said. They were a procession of hotel rooms, with television and radio programs muttering or screaming through the bedroom walls. They were places where she was required to be dynamic and to look attractive, and to give the impression that she was delighted to crusade for this cause. Although, since that day nearly a week ago, when she had telephoned to find out if the children were all right and had heard that Angus was back in Fond Port, she had constantly carried the sickening knowledge in her mind that for him this journey of hers would be the last straw, the final insult.

He did not want to be with her, but that would not excuse her absence. To him it would seem monstrous that she would leave her home and the children for this. This, Clare would think, looking around the current hotel room. The clerk had said, "It hasn't been made up, madam, but you can go up if you wish." And here she was with the whisky bottles and the newspapers left by the last occupants, and the corn plasters on the bathroom floor.

For this, she would say to herself, taking her place in the glare over the speakers' table, mechanically admiring the stupid arrangements of hard little chrysanthemums, and trying to remember the name of the woman who was going to introduce her so that she could be polite in acknowledgment. For this witless conversation about Bermuda with a stranger who was trying to impress her with social connections.

To be home, she would think, would be heaven. To decide to put the Venetian bowl on the table for a change and to fill it with white and yellow grapes. To tell the cook to be careful with the curry and ask Magda to use the tear-drop glasses for the martinis because Angus likes them best. To make the children go to bed now—but their devices to stay up longer are always so enchanting.

But it isn't that way any longer, remember that. Remember it hard and deep, and cruelly. This will settle it for Angus. This will show him.

She had given happiness up for another silly interview for some newspaper.

"How did you first become interested in birth control, Mrs. Baird?"

"You have four children? Well, evidently you don't believe entirely in birth control."

Try to explain again that you do not want to annihilate families.

"Do you spend a great deal of your time lecturing? Do you find that it interferes with family life?"

Say no—say it brightly. Tell the monstrous lie.

"Some women think that birth control will result in an increase of cancer of the uterus. What is your opinion?"

Often the smirks that the subject of her talks would bring to women's faces nauseated Clare. Sometimes the hostility she saw in other faces was almost frightening. Women should not hate like that. Women with such expressions wrote the kind of letters that Angus had read about her.

But she had fulfilled her commitments, followed the schedule, and she knew with a kind of horror that she had been successful. They would want her to do this again. Because she attracted large audiences. Because her voice was clear over the microphone. Because women liked her clothes. Because she was socially prominent and her picture had been in *Town and Country*. So often the audiences were large for the wrong reasons.

"It was just a wonderful talk—and you looked so beautiful!"

"My cousin is married to Kitty Allerdice and I know Kitty is a friend of yours. . . ."

"I love dark mink. . . ."

Now, in the air terminal, Clare lifted her weary shoulders under the dark mink and went again to the information desk.

"Have you any idea how long the planes going north will be grounded?"

"We're hoping that the weather will improve, madam. Any change will be announced."

It was a three-hour flight to Fond Port. Her plane had been scheduled to leave at noon, but it was nearly six o'clock in the evening now. She had refrained from telephoning her house during the afternoon because of the uncertainty, and she did not want to keep the chauffeur waiting indefinitely at the airport. Now if she telephoned, Angus might be home. He might pick up the phone and she would hear the chill in his voice.

I cannot bear it, Clare said to herself. It was dreadful before, but to go back to it is worse. What will we do about the children? He is so proud of Gus. Gus is old enough to miss his father—he would always miss him. But the children must stay together. There must be one control—one protection. I will never let my children be passed back and forth between us, to be bewildered, to grow cynical.

Perhaps I couldn't have the children. They might not let me have them. I am the one who is to blame. That's what anyone—any outsider—would think. My husband asked me to give up a position and a connection. And any normal woman

181

would have done it, even if she fretted a little and did it against her will. But she would have done it because her husband wanted her to, especially if criticism of her was bad for his business. I've been quite unnatural. A judge would say so—there would actually be a judge deciding about us!

She paced the smooth floors of the terminal building where they were not crowded with irritated, thwarted passengers, and her thoughts walked with her. When she came to a wall in her walk or her thinking, she retraced the same path. Once she ordered a cup of coffee in one of the open restaurants and that took a little time. She looked over the toys in the gift shop and bought a few small things that would fit into her handbag. They made it very heavy and her wrist ached. She sat down on one of the long smooth benches and wished that she could lie flat on its smoothness and sleep and sleep and not be herself any more.

I was the one who broke up our life together. It was a beautiful life. I loved it. I didn't want to smash it, to hurt Angus. Why did I do it? Sometimes I forget. If I had another chance—if I could turn time back to that morning when he asked me to resign and go down to the lodge and hide—what would I do?

I'd do the same thing over again, she thought in despair. I would have to, because my life—our happiness—isn't everything. I'm too tired and mixed up to figure it out. But something would click in me and I'd know, if I had to do it again.

"Announcing the departure of Flight 112 from Gate Six in the North Concourse. All aboard please . . ."

That was her flight. Clare hurried to the gate.

On the plane she soon fell asleep from utter exhaustion, but when some mental call woke her and she looked at her watch, apprehension rushed over her again. In less than a half hour she would arrive in Fond Port. And Angus was there. For a minute sheer delight at the thought of seeing him was stronger than the fear of the meeting. Then she began to plan it. I will take a taxi home, enter the house very quietly. I have my key—and I will act as if everything is normal. The children are in bed by this time and asleep. I'll not wake them, just look at them. And I will try to act tonight as if things are as they used to be. Perhaps I could make him remember, feel like that—I won't let there be any argument. I won't mention what I've been doing. I will not bring trouble into our house tonight.

Angus may not be there. If he knows I'm coming, he may have gone out to the club or somewhere. Is it possible I've become the kind of woman who drives her husband out of his house? But perhaps he doesn't know I'm coming. The nurse has my schedule, but he may not have even asked about it.

". . . until the plane comes to a full stop," said the stewardess.

Now it was stopped. Clare drew the mink coat closer— she needed protection from more than the cold now—and went down the aisle, down the steps. She came into the light of the runways with her head held high, because that was the only way she could hold it. Then her heart turned over, for she saw him.

There she is. She is safe. She is here. Angus came through the gate, past the prohibiting signs, careless of breaking the rules. There was no barrier that could keep him from her a minute longer. The relief that filled him was intoxicating, the joy unbelievable. For the hours of waiting and fearing had been torture. The delay, the dangerous weather, the terrible thought that he would not have another chance had piled one apprehension upon another. Worst of all, as the plane had come in for landing, was the fear that she might not be on it. But she had come.

He kissed her. Again. It had been a long thirst.

The official who had followed to reprimand the man who had broken out of the waiting crowd stepped back without doing it. This was something special, an emergency. He could see that.

"You must have had a terrible day, Clare. We've been getting reports."

"The delay was tiresome. But have you been waiting long? I didn't expect . . ."

"I couldn't not be here."

"I'm so glad you're home, Angus!"

"So am I," he said. "God, so am I."

He led her across the runway. As they went into the waiting room she realized that he was walking like any boy with his girl. He was holding her hand in public.

Chapter 16

❧❧❧

Dr. Helm said, "I have not told your sister. She believes that she cannot take the child home at present only because the birth was premature and it must stay in the incubator."

"Does Christopher know?"

"Yes, of course. From the first. And he plans to tell Joyce when she is back in her normal surroundings. He may have done so by this time. He thinks that with the other children around to comfort her, she may not take this as hard as she might otherwise. I hope so."

Anne looked through the window of the incubator at the miniature figure. The top of its head was covered. As she watched, it moved a tiny hand.

"This is the first time I have seen her. The nurses wouldn't let me before. I'm glad you were here today, Doctor. The baby looks all right. She's pretty."

"They sometimes look fine."

"Isn't there a possibility that the place in her head may close?"

"Not in this case. The aperture is too large."

"And that means . . ."

"That brain development will never be normal."

Anne shuddered. "Will she live?"

The doctor said gruffly, "Sometimes they do. For years. Sometimes only a few weeks."

"What caused it, Dr. Helm?"

"We don't know. It happens in a certain proportion of births."

"Can it have been because Joyce had too many children? Too fast?"

"That and overactivity at home may have caused the birth to be premature. But not the other condition, so far as we know."

"I don't know how she can manage. Her hands are so full now."

Dr. Helm said, "That is why I am very glad to have this chance to speak to you about this. Joyce must not get any notion that she can bring this child home and take care of it herself. There are places where such cases are cared for, and I'll take that up with Christopher at the proper time. If the child lives. If you can, try to keep Joyce from being morbid. During her confinement she kept talking about hoping that she wouldn't be 'punished.' Of course she was under sedation, but I think that there may be some religious quirk in her mind. She's very pious. I hope too that, if you have influence with her, you will strongly advise Joyce not to have more children."

"But you said this wasn't because she's had so many—"

"I did—and it's possible that Joyce might have a healthy seven-pounder next time. But there shouldn't be a next time. It's too unlikely."

"Have you told her she shouldn't have any more?"

"I told her that several years ago. Her priest overrules me, I'm afraid."

"They can't take care of any more children. Christopher does his best but . . ."

"It's up to Christopher," said the doctor with no sympathy

186

in his voice. "Well, young lady, I'm sorry to have to tell you this. I'm extremely fond of your sister. She's a good girl, a brave girl. But you get her not to take the pitcher to the well again, if you can."

As he had been talking to her, the doctor was being paged over the loudspeaker and now, after a touch of reassurance on Anne's shoulder, he went down the hospital corridor. Anne stood looking at the baby through the window, feeling with acute pain that someone should love that small living being, thinking that Christopher and Joyce had no right to bring a child into the world and abandon it. But what could they do? What could anyone do?

Joyce had gone home from the hospital the day before, and because she had not been allowed to see her child, Anne had suspected that something was wrong. The nurses had been evasive, but when she had come to the hospital today, she had been fortunate in finding Dr. Helm there. Now she knew the truth. It was going to be hard to face Joyce, and Anne was on her way to the Hawley house now.

Christopher was home when Anne arrived. He looked gray-faced, unkempt and very tired. She thought with pity, Chris used to be so handsome, such a charmer.

"Good," he said at the sight of Anne, "Joyce will be glad to see you. She's up in her room resting, and I've told these little monsters that they must pipe down and not disturb her."

Most of the little monsters were parked before the television set in the living room. Anne stepped over and around them and went to the kitchen to speak to Lena Johnson, whom she had hired to take care of the house while Joyce was in the hospital. Dinner was cooking fragrantly, and the baby was in her high chair beside Lena, splashing her spoon in a dish of cereal.

Sammy came rushing to Anne when she started to go upstairs and shouted, "Mom's up there! She's come home! She told a lie. She promised to bring—"

"Shut up, Sam," said his father, following him and catching the child by the neck of his torn sweater, "do you want a licking?" And with worry, "Try to cheer her up, Anne, will you?"

Anne asked, "She knows? You've told her?"

Christopher nodded. "I had to. She sort of knew anyway. She guessed. Kept asking questions. I thought we'd better get it over with."

Anne went upstairs and very cautiously opened the door of the bedroom that Joyce and Christopher shared. Her sister was lying on the bed, so motionless that at first Anne thought she was asleep. But she turned her head and said, "Chris?"

"No, it's me, Joyce. How does it feel to be home?"

"Wonderful. They were all so glad to see me. And Lena has taught the baby to feed herself."

"So I saw! There's one more milestone passed."

"You're awfully good to pay Lena, Anne. Chris is going to see that you get the money back, of course. He insists on that. But this month so many expenses piled up—"

"Look, Lena is a birthday present. If you insist, I'll wrap her up in tissue paper and tie a ribbon around her. If I can find enough ribbon to circle those mighty thighs."

Joyce smiled faintly. "Anne, you're a dear. But Anne, do you know that I couldn't bring the baby home? And Sammy was so disappointed."

"Sammy's disappointment is the least of my worries," said Anne cheerfully.

"He's very sensitive—it seemed almost that he sensed what happened. I told him I couldn't bring the baby just yet. But"— her very voice darkened—"Chris says I can't bring her home at all. She's . . ."

"I know about it, Joyce. I saw Dr. Helm and he told me."

"They didn't even let me see her!"

That was best, thought Anne. You would never forget

188

the pathos of that tiny face—or that covered head. I must never let Joyce know that I saw her.

She said, "With premature babies they have to be very careful."

"She's not just premature—she's not normal. She's never going to be normal. God punished me, all right."

"What nonsense are you talking?"

"I didn't want that baby. I pretended I did—I said so. But I didn't want another child."

"That was perfectly natural. You have a big family—you can't take care of more children. You haven't the strength."

"But you shouldn't resent a gift from God," said Joyce drearily, "and I did. Sometimes I almost hoped—"

"Stop it, Joyce," Anne said gently but decisively, "stop thinking ridiculous things. You had the baby and you went through it bravely."

"If I ever have the chance to bring another soul—"

"Did the doctor give you anything to make you sleep?" Anne interrupted.

"I guess so."

"Where is it?"

"The blue ones in the bottle on the dressing table."

"I want you to take one now. Dr. Helm said that I should see that you did." Anne brought a pill and a glass of water to her sister. Joyce looked up, her lovely eyes misty with tears.

"They baptized her. Christopher said so. She's named after me. Mary Joyce, my full name—remember how Grandmother used to call me that because she said every Catholic had to have a saint's name and Joyce was heathen?"

"I remember." She's so lovely, thought Anne. And she's morbid. I must talk to Christopher.

She said, "Joyce, please think of those delightful rowdy characters downstairs and how much they need you. Now lie quietly—you'll soon be asleep."

Christopher was in the dining room, pouring himself a drink.

He said, "I certainly need this tonight. Have one with me?"

"No, I'm driving and I have to cover a dinner meeting at the Pacific Hotel tonight. Need all my wits."

"How is she?"

"You mustn't let her get morbid, Chris."

"I know. I'm doing my best."

"It's terribly disappointing—but don't let her blame herself."

"This happens once in ten thousand births, the doctor told me. And this time it had to be us."

"You have other children."

"I didn't actually want this one," said Chris gloomily, "if you want to know the truth about it."

The wretched little unwanted waif, thought Anne, and saw it in memory.

She said, "Joyce shouldn't have any more children, Chris. She isn't up to it."

"So help me God, she won't," said Chris, "and no priest is going to make me believe that she has to!"

But Joyce may make you believe it, thought Anne. Or you'll have too many drinks and it will happen again.

Christopher refilled his glass. "They ought to do something about it," he said, "the priests, or the bishops—or the Pope. How's a decent Catholic that plays the rules they lay down going to get ahead? How's he going to compete?"

"I don't know."

"How are you and Francis Dearborn going to work it out?" he asked. "I mean about having kids."

"We aren't," said Anne. "We don't see each other any more. Fran and I called it a day. We aren't going to be married."

"What happened?"

"He didn't like a picture of me that was in the paper and I didn't like his attitude."

190

"You'll make it up."

"Not possibly."

"Sure you aren't making a mistake? Dearborn is the type that's going to go a long way."

"I suppose he will," said Anne, "but he's not going in my direction."

The children in the next room were laughing. Joyce would be almost asleep now. And Chris had his drinks to dull his worries. For the hour it was warm and safe here.

"No thanks," said Anne again to Christopher's offer of a drink, "I must be on my way. I'll be out again tomorrow or next day. And Chris, Joyce must keep this woman in the kitchen for a few weeks until she gets her strength back. I want you to insist on that."

"I don't like the idea of you paying the help in this house. It's just a loan, you know."

"It's the least an old-maid sister can do."

"And we can't have you an old maid," said Christopher.

"The unmarried state is a solution to a lot of things."

"Not a good-looking girl like you," insisted Christopher, now a little incoherent. "It's an awful lot of grief, Anne, but it's a whole lot of fun too. Better make it up with Fran Dearborn."

They could never make it up. When she looked back on her relationship with Francis Dearborn now, she saw that for some time it had been fraying under the attraction and desire they had for each other. That had lasted longer than anything else. The threads of agreement on impersonal things had pulled apart, and interest in each other's work wore out, and finally trust gave way. There was nothing left except the tingling of sex and the pride that resisted giving up a personal conquest.

On her way to her assignment at the Pacific Hotel Anne let herself remember that final quarrel. She had thrust the memory of it under her preoccupation with Joyce's family during the last two weeks, but Christopher's probing brought it to the surface of her mind again.

She had hoped that Francis would not see that picture of her in the paper. She herself had looked for it the next day with some dread, and found it printed along with an account of Pearl Lemoy's murder and a photograph of Luke Lemoy wearing handcuffs. The caption read *Commissioner Porada Visits Home of Murdered Reliefer*. Anne was not identified by name, for the newspaper would not advertise a reporter for a rival sheet. But it was a clear-cut picture of herself and Porada, with his hand on her arm protectively. Anne was bareheaded and looked excited and pretty.

Francis called her early in the same evening.

"I want to see you, Anne," he said abruptly.

"Tonight? I was going out to the Hawleys. . . ."

"I must see you. It's very important. I'm coming up." It was not a request but a demand. Then he asked, sharply, "Are you alone?"

"Why yes."

"I'm having something to eat downtown, and then I'll be there."

When he came into her sitting room, he did not try to kiss her. He looked at her as if he were a judge passing sentence and said, "I've been very deeply shocked. You know of course that your picture is in the evening paper with Porada and a bunch of criminals."

"They had no right to take that picture. I was annoyed too."

"I warned you that such a thing might happen."

"It isn't serious—the murder is awful, but the silly picture doesn't matter."

"It matters very much to me."

"Oh Fran, please don't fuss about it. The Lemoy affair is painful enough."

"I'll say it is—it's very painful for a man to see a girl whom he has honored and respected and intends to marry in the company of criminals."

"I wasn't in Luke Lemoy's company! Don't you pity those poor people—that woman—and the boy who's marked for life?"

"Those hoodlums aren't my responsibility," he said, "but I have felt that you were. What is going on between you and this man Porada?"

"Nothing is going on."

"That's what you told me. And the next thing I know is that you're in a newspaper picture with him hanging on to you."

"He was trying to make me duck the photographers. He drove me out to the Lemoy house to see if there was anything to be done for the family."

"He had the nerve to ask you to do that!"

"No, I asked him. I was concerned about the children."

"But they're nothing to you."

She sighed, "I suppose they aren't."

"Anne, this kind of thing has got to stop."

"What kind of thing?"

"I won't have a girl I'm going to marry mixed up with a publicity hound like Porada and running around the slums with him!"

"Please listen, Fran—"

"I don't want excuses. And to be fair I don't believe you got into this mess intentionally. I've given the whole situation a lot of thought—not just tonight—because I've been disturbed for some time. I've seen where all this was leading. There's just one thing to do. We'll get married immediately, turn over a new leaf and forget this. Begin to build ourselves up. The first thing to do is to get you out of this newspaper racket before you lose your good name."

"I'm not in any danger of that."

"I don't think you're the best judge of that."

"Anyway, I've told you that we can't be married until I see Joyce through this confinement."

"I'm going to put my foot down on that," he said, "put it down hard. If Chris Hawley breeds kids like rabbits, let him look after them. I'm not going to permit—"

"That's a strange word."

"It's the right word when a girl is making a fool of herself and dragging the man she's going to marry along with her."

"You're not going to marry me," said Anne, "you're going to be spared that contamination."

He said, "I was only trying to make it clear—"

"You have," she said. "You've made it clear that you would expect anyone who marries you to be selfish, snobbish, indifferent to anyone else she might love except you, unable to meet interesting people or to be seen with them—you've made that all very clear."

"I suppose by interesting people you mean Porada."

"I might."

"How far have you really gone with him?" he asked. "I know you—and I know you have it in you to—"

"That's enough," she said, as if she struck him in the mouth. "Get out of here. I never want to see you again."

She found a place for her car and went into the Pacific Hotel. She disliked this assignment tonight because she would see Carl Porada again. She had tried to turn it over to someone else, but Max Fleming had refused.

He had said, "No, I'll send someone else to the Ice Follies and you cover the dinner of that birth control outfit. Porada is the main speaker at it, and he may shoot off some fireworks. It's right up your street, Anne. You've got the background."

She couldn't refuse to go. There was no reason to be self-conscious or embarrassed, anyway. She told herself, a man always expects to kiss a girl good night when he takes her home. He thought nothing of it and neither did I.

She took her place at the familiar press table as the men and women who were to be seated on the dais were coming into the ballroom. Several ministers. A well-known doctor. The trustees of the local association. Clare Baird. Mrs. Angus Baird was very beautiful tonight in a black sheath. And beside her walked Carl Porada, scowling a little. His scowl is just a cover-up—he's really very friendly, thought Anne. He looks very tall on the platform and so humanly awkward.

Clare Baird looks much better than she did when I saw her at the clinic. It's not just the lights. She's glowing again. She has a radiance that gives you a lift when you look at her. Carl must think she is wonderful. Of course, he and Clare Baird believe in the same things, they're both convinced. That's very important to him. He could never understand that a person can be confused, pulled two ways at the same time.

Carl Porada saw Anne and lifted his hand to salute her, with his sudden, complete smile. Anne knew that he said something about her to Clare Baird, for she too singled Anne out with apparent pleasure. But Anne tried to imply in her response to their recognition that she would take no advantage of it. She was here on a job, as a working girl. Never had she felt more lonely, less attractive. She did not look toward the head table again and was very glad when the dinner finally came to an end and with great charm and poise Clare Baird came to the microphone.

There were no fireworks set off by Carl Porada. He spoke intelligently but not with brilliant oratory. As he talked, Anne remembered their strange encounters, the unexpected drive, the sight of the house that was his and that she had praised without knowing that. She remembered him pushing the cart around the supermarket and talking to the priest. I wish I could see that priest again, thought Anne. Carl was impressed. He said that Father Walker spoke the King's English. He was a gentle priest. I wonder what he was able to do for Luke Lemoy. Carl would know, but I will never call Carl up again. Especially not after breaking with Fran. She thought, if I went to see Father Walker to find out what happened to the boy, I could ask him some questions. I could tell him why I don't think I'll stay in the Church. I have to talk to somebody.

Chapter 17

∾✦∾

When Anne was a child, her grandmother had taken her several times on some errand to the house of the parish priest, and she had never forgotten how it looked or how uncomfortable she had been in its atmosphere. The living room, which was all she ever saw of the inside of the house, was so stiffly furnished that it seemed barren. There was a large colored picture of the Pope dominating one wall and a huge crucifix on another. The chairs were polished, uncushioned and difficult. If she sat at all, it was on the very edge of one. That was what Anne expected Father Walker's house would be like.

But the impulse she had felt at the banquet to talk to the priest had not faded away overnight. It had become stronger. The sight of the infant in the hospital haunted her. Her mental rebellion against the unyielding doctrine of the Church made her restless and distrait. She had to talk to someone, she told herself. She had to fight this out with someone, declare herself, clarify what she believed. When her work was finished in the afternoon, she had found the address of Father Walker in the telephone book and come to his house.

He was home and must have been writing at a shabby table desk under a window in his living room, for papers and open books were spread upon it. There was no servant. Father Walker opened the door for her and said that of course he remembered her. He told her pleasantly that he was very glad to see her again and invited her to come in. He made her coming here easy for her, as did his surprising room.

There was no luxury in it and not much furniture. But the rug was pink and red, worn down to the warp in some places, and obviously an old Persian one. One chair was low, another deep, and small tables beside each of them held ashtrays. On one wall there was an extraordinary painting, in colors as subtle as those in the Oriental rug.

"What a nice room," she said.

"Well, there are always a few *lares* and *penates* that make living pleasanter for each of us," said Father Walker. "We can get along without them, but we don't want to. My poor shabby rug belonged to my grandmother and where I go it goes. So far anyway."

"The painting is fascinating."

"A young friend of mine in Ecuador was the artist."

"They're Indians," she said, studying it.

"Yes. It's called *Una Noche en El Guinche* and this is its story. El Guinche is the Lourdes of Ecuador, and on a certain feast day miracles are hoped for in the Church. This picture is very true to life. I've often seen them like this, the square before the church full of their curved bodies on the ground waiting for the church to open, the calloused bare heels—and there is always a squat Indian woman with a baby on her back —just like that."

"It's pathetic."

"Not entirely—they're full of hope. A miracle may happen."

"Superstition, isn't it, Father?"

He said, "The line between superstition and faith is sometimes a very fine one. Take this chair. And won't you have a cigarette?"

"Thank you. Father Walker, I wanted to inquire about

198

Luke Lemoy, and I was sure that you would know what's happening in his case."

"The report isn't good news. He may always be dangerous. His mother's habits—you know what they were?"

"Yes."

"They gave him a horror of sex. That was back of his homicidal outburst. It could happen again. There's not much of an outlook for Luke in this world."

"He should never have come into it, of course. He should never have been born."

"That's not for us to know," said Father Walker, "nor to decide."

"Isn't it? When a boy, born in such circumstances as Luke was, will obviously never have a chance?"

"When Jenny talked to me about you after that night, she told me that you were a Catholic, as I recall it," he answered obliquely.

"I am, Father. That's what I'm up against. It's why I came to see you today. I did want to know about Luke, but that wasn't the only reason. I couldn't talk to the pastor of my own parish because he—well, he rubs me the wrong way."

The priest gave her an almost mischievous grin. "We priests all do that," he said, "to one or another. So it's lucky that we vary in temperament. You are as welcome here as if you were one of my parishioners, and it's more than possible that one of mine may seek the priest who rubs you the wrong way. What is it you want to talk to me about?"

Anne plunged into it.

"Father, my sister has just had a defective child. If it lives it will be . . . an idiot."

"Poor woman. Has she other children?"

"She has six others."

"Then she's greatly blessed. Are they healthy?"

"The older ones are. Not the last two. Father Walker, she shouldn't keep on having children. The doctor says that. But she's a devout Catholic. She thinks the condition of this last child is a punishment from God because she didn't want to have it."

"That's hysteria."

"Of course it is. But Father Walker, when there are cases like Luke Lemoy and babies born like that one of my sister's—how can the Church be so rigid about birth control? It's cruel and unreasonable. It's driving me out of the Church."

"The worry for your sister?"

"Not just that."

"I thought not."

Anne said, "I'm confused. I feel like a hypocrite because I go to church and yet I think that the people who are working for birth control aren't wrong. I think Carl Porada is right—for example, in his plan for nurses to teach it. I've had to stop going to Communion because I felt I didn't have any right to receive the Sacrament. That tears me to pieces because I have nothing to tie to any more or give me peace. No place to pray when awful things like this baby happen. I love the Church. It's my Church and they haven't any right to drive me out of it!"

"That won't happen."

"I'm afraid that it will."

"Are you yourself contemplating marriage?"

"No. I was more or less engaged, but that's broken off."

"You were engaged to Mr. Porada?"

"Oh no—he wasn't the one! It was quite another person. A Catholic." Anne gave a mirthless little laugh. "Carl Porada would never want to have his life hampered by a Catholic."

"I don't want to be intrusive. But this other man—who you tell me is a Catholic—did you break with him for the reasons we have been discussing?"

"No, not entirely—though it was one of the reasons I began to see him as he was. He meant to do what he pleased about practicing birth control and to stay in the Church, anyway."

"Too many of them are like that," said the priest thoughtfully.

"The Church is to blame for it. If it's so unwilling to face modern conditions, so unable to change . . ."

"It is not unwilling to change. And the Church faces the fact that modern families should be limited. It admits that."

"By rhythm? How can the Church expect that ignorant people—those Indians in your picture, for example—will practice rhythm? Or continence?"

"Other methods may be found that are acceptable to our religion."

"Father, I've heard it said hundreds of times—the natural law can't be changed."

"None the less ways may be found."

She was silently skeptical, and as if he knew that, he went on in quiet persuasion.

"They will be found if people like yourself—who love the Church as you show me you do—stay within it and are faithful even when that is very difficult. The Church needs and loves its docile members—like your sister. It also needs and loves its critics, if they will trust it and are obedient even as they search for changes that will not be destructive. But you must have patience."

"You really believe that a solution will be found?"

"I know that it will. I do not know when. But even if methods of birth control are found which do not break the natural law, even if the natural law should be reinterpreted so that methods now forbidden become acceptable to the Church, we shall not have reached the millennium."

She was listening without resistance now.

"You must not forget," said the priest, "that the Church is the guardian of marriage and the guardian of love. Marriage is becoming weak in love, for it is presently overmaterialistic. Love is being constantly degraded to identification with sexual practices instead of mirroring divine love in its human manifestations as it should. There is a canticle of love." He repeated it slowly and without affectation, lingering on the words, " 'Love is swift, sincere, pleasant and delightful. Love is strong, patient, courageous, long-suffering. Love feels no burdens, values no labors, would willingly do more than it can—where he who loves not faints and lies down.' "

He smiled at her. "Will you remember all that when you marry? That planning your family is important, but only part of it?"

"I'll remember that even though I never marry," said Anne.

Chapter 18

~~~~~~

"When I called this number the first time," said Carl
Porada, "it was to ask a favor. And now I'm doing the same
thing again. But I promise that this will be the last time. I
won't let it become a habit."

"What's the favor?" asked Anne.

"I want you to take a look at my house on the lake shore.
I need some advice. You said you more or less admired its
location, and I would like very much to have you see the
inside and tell me what you think of it. If it seems to you a
livable place. I'm thinking of disposing of it."

"I couldn't buy it. I'm not in the market." Did he imagine
he could sell it to her and Francis Dearborn, she wondered.

"Of course not. That wasn't what I had in mind at all. I
just want your opinion of the place—to have you give me your
judgment of what its value as a home might be. I know it's
very nervy of me to ask you to do it—don't give it a thought
if it seems a bore or a nuisance."

She remembered that he had told her that the girl he had
bought it for didn't like it. She had shaken his confidence in
his own judgment.

"I'd love to see your house, Carl," said Anne.

"Thank you," he said, "that's wonderful. Can I pick you up at about the same time as I did that other Sunday?"

"That will be fine."

It was an unusual and rather ingenuous request, thought Anne. But men often did like a woman's opinion about furnishings, and he thought she was going to marry Francis and would be interested in such things. She told herself that it would be a way to fill this empty Sunday afternoon, and it would be interesting to find out how his campaign was going.

But that did not account for her rising excitement or for the critical way she looked at herself in the mirror and considered what to wear. She thought, I've been letting myself go lately, not caring enough about how I look. At the hotel the other night Carl must have thought I was a pitiful contrast to Clare Baird. I'll wear the yellow wool suit this afternoon. I've never had it on since I bought it. I bought it to dazzle Fran and then I stopped wanting to dazzle him and thought I might as well save it for a special occasion.

If the yellow suit impressed Carl Porada, he did not say so. His eager glance covered her in his complete way, but he seemed almost preoccupied at first. He put her into his car and she felt that it was a curiously familiar place to be. Carl seemed to read her thought.

"Like old times," he said.

"Only two old times."

"Is that all? Seems like more. I often think of you there. I called you several times after that night we went to the Lemoys. But you were never home."

"My sister has been sick. I was at her house very often when I wasn't at the newspaper."

"I'm sorry to hear that. Is she better now?"

"Much better."

"What I called you about was that picture of us in the newspaper. To ask if it upset you. Did you see it?"

"Yes, I saw it," she said indifferently.

204

"I hope it didn't embarrass you or anything."

"There was no reason why it should," she said rather coldly, thinking of Francis Dearborn's reaction.

"Of course, you're used to publicity."

"Not so used as you must be. You're all over the papers these days. How are things going?"

"We'll hire that nurse. I put that much over. Whether they'll throw me out of office in May because of it I don't know."

"I hope not."

"Thanks. That means a lot to me, Anne."

"Are you really going to sell your house?"

"That depends. You can tell me if I should."

"I'm no interior decorator."

"It's not an interior decorator's opinion that I want."

They reached the lake shore and saw gay waves sparkling in the sun.

"The lake is in blue and wearing her diamonds," said Anne.

"That's a pretty thought. You have lots of them, don't you?"

"I have some that aren't so pretty."

"Don't have any that aren't today."

"All right, I won't. I'll try anyway. There's your fine house. Why didn't you tell me it was yours when I first saw it?"

"I don't know really. I wondered about that. It didn't seem the time."

He swung the car into the driveway beside it, and when he opened the front door with his key the spaniels came rushing to them.

"Hello, boys," said Anne. "They must be a lot of fun." She rubbed the head of one of them and the other came jealously for the same treatment.

"They don't often do that with strangers," said Carl admiringly. "Shall we go in?"

He stepped back to let her precede him and she went ahead,

hoping that she was going to be able to praise the place, to say something encouraging. She looked around and then turned to him with an almost puzzled look.

"Why Carl, it's lovely!"

"You think it's all right?"

"Who wouldn't? Wherever did you get those rugs?"

"The man who built the house found a Swede woman who made them on her own loom. I've always sort of liked them."

"And that fireplace—and the chairs. Danish?"

"That's right."

She went from one thing to another while he laid a fire of birch logs and lit it.

"Want to see the rest of the place?"

"Every inch of it."

He saved the master's bedroom to the last of her inspection, then opened that door. She took a few steps and stopped, looking at the broad bed on the dais, at the curtainless window that needed no curtains, at the lake beyond.

"What imagination," she said softly, "what a place to sleep and wake. Carl, it would be a shame to give this house up. You'll never find another like it in the world. How could that girl not like it!"

"I am very, very glad that she didn't." He took Anne's hand and led her out of the bedroom and back to the room where the fire was leaping over the logs.

"Please sit down and let me look at you for a minute," he said, and his voice was grave. Suddenly Anne found that she was trembling. She took the chair he offered but did not look at him.

"Anne, you know why I asked you to come here, don't you?"

She did now. She had not allowed herself to know it until this minute, because she might be wrong. And because it was impossible.

"I wanted you to see this house because I want you to live

in it with me. I love you very much, Anne. I want to marry you. That's how it is. That's all of it."

"You hardly know me, Carl."

"I know you very well. I would have asked you to marry me that night we went to the Lemoy place. I was sure of how I felt then, but from what you said I thought you were engaged to Dearborn, that you'd chosen him. When I looked at you the other night in the hotel I was sick at the thought of what I couldn't have. Then there was a miracle. Just last night I was in a restaurant and I saw Dearborn there with a girl who wasn't you. He was not being casual. He was holding her hand, cuddling up to her. And I thought, I won't let him have Anne."

"He never will. There wasn't any reason why he shouldn't be holding the girl's hand. There's nothing between him and me now."

"Nothing?"

"No—that was settled weeks ago."

"Are you unhappy about it?"

"It wouldn't have been a good marriage."

"Like my mistake. Then we found each other and there's no mistake. Anne, don't you think we could make a good marriage?"

"I wish I did. But I don't think so, Carl."

"Why not? Don't you like me?"

She flashed her answer in a straight glance, but when he came toward her she pushed back her chair and stood at a distance rather desperately.

"Carl, I'm a Catholic."

"I know you are—what of it? Does it make me impossible for you because I'm not?"

"It makes me impossible for you."

"I don't know what you mean."

Anne said, "My sister Joyce has had seven children and the last one is defective. Would you like to have seven children?"

"It would be quite a family."

"For most people it's too large a family. I wouldn't want that many."

"We don't have to go that far then."

"But we might. Because I'm a Catholic—and as long as I'm one—I can't use artificial birth control. Nothing else is certain to prevent having children."

"I know that. But—I can. The man can."

"Not with me."

"But people do work it out that way, Anne."

"I know. But I couldn't. It would be cheating. This is horrid, clinical conversation. It probably repels you. But I've thought and thought about it. I've even imagined what would happen if you did come to care for me and we married. Before long you'd think me a pious fool, frightened of the priests. But that's not what it is. I went to see Father Walker—you remember that priest who was at the Lemoy house that night?"

"Very well. I liked him."

"He thinks there may be changes some day in what the Church allows. He's just as disturbed as you are—and as Clare Baird is about children who aren't wanted or properly cared for. But he made me feel stronger about my religion than I've ever felt in my life. I would never be happy if I gave it up. But I can't cheat. I'd cheat myself. He made me feel the depth of love, and that the demands it makes and what it has to bear are part of it. To you this must be meaningless."

"Meaningless? Nothing ever meant more. I never thought I could be so proud of anyone as I am of you right now. You're brave and you're honest. Now let me say my blundering piece. I love you. I want children—as many as you would want to bear. But I want you more. I want you more than sex. In my house. In my life always. If it means that I have to get along without part of you for short times—or long times, if it seems best—I can do that. You have to take my word for that. Anne, sex is only part of it. But life with you is the whole thing."

"Love is," said Anne, and opened her arms in a gesture she had never made before.

Father Walker was at his desk. He was writing the ending of a little book on married life which he had been working on for a long time in the hope that it would be useful and comforting.

He wrote,

The vine must be fruitful if possible. For good fruit is needed. But the husbandman must take great care in its cultivation lest the vine wither. Nor should he seed his olive plants so closely that they are in danger of not attaining full growth.